AFTER THE WAR

TOM PALMER

Conkers

FOREWORD

A group of young people arrived in the Lake District in the summer of 1945 and stayed for a few months, the last of them leaving in early 1946. Although they only spent a short time in the area, it was a profoundly important experience for them, and they made a big impression on those who met them at the time.

In 2005 I became intrigued by references that were made to these youngsters, and when I began to investigate, a truly remarkable story emerged.

People I spoke to initially in the immediate area had different opinions as to who these children had been. They were variously described as being part of the Kindertransport, children on holiday from London, German prisoners of war, and in one case they were thought to have been children from Holland escaping famine. All these suggestions turned out to have some basis in fact but almost all had missed the crucial point.

The young people were in fact Jewish child survivors of the Holocaust and, moreover, they had arrived in the Lake District directly from the concentration camps.

To say that I was astonished would be an understatement.

Talking to these Jewish children many years later, and to more and more local people, I began to compile recollections, often handed down from parents and grandparents, that painted a picture of both human compassion and also the ability of people to recover from even the most horrendous experiences. These memories became the basis for the Lake District Holocaust Project, established in 2013.

When Tom Palmer approached me to ask if he could write a book about the Jewish children and their stay in the Lake District, I was immediately taken by his desire to totally immerse himself in the story. We worked with him on this extraordinary book project and he was always full of the same compassion as those who helped the children in their early days of recovery.

He was also utterly dedicated to doing the story justice, and I am sure you will see that he has. It is a story from the past, told in the present, with lessons for us all for the future.

Trevor Avery BEM

Lake District Holocaust Project

(Photograph on previous page: Some of the children on a boat trip on Windermere.)

ONE

Even though he was afraid, Yossi forced himself to crawl to the window in the side of the aeroplane. There were no seats, so he had to crouch and stay on all fours as he and the other passengers were thrown about by the turbulence.

Outside he could see a wall of white and a wing wobbling so hard it looked like it might fall off.

Behind him, Yossi heard children cry out, the sound of at least one person being sick. And some laughter too.

"Come and sit down here, Yossi," a woman's voice called out.

Yossi did as he was told, scrambling along the floor of the Stirling bomber to rejoin the other children and adults sitting on blankets.

Yossi loved aeroplanes. He should have been scared of them, as the first time he'd seen one, six years ago at the beginning of the war, a German bomber had tried to destroy his home town in Poland. Then, over the following years, he'd seen bombs falling from British and American aeroplanes, targeting the factories where he was forced to work.

But he still loved them, perhaps because aeroplanes were a sign that change was coming. And once he was in the concentration camps, Yossi was desperate for change. He was also fascinated by these powerful machines. How could a huge piece of metal with all these people on board take off and then land without breaking into pieces?

He glanced at the faces of the two boys closest to him. Didn't it worry them?

The boys in question were called Mordecai and Leo. Both of them were fifteen years old, like Yossi. And both seemed to be focusing so hard on what they were doing that they were barely aware of bouncing around in the clouds.

Mordecai, short with dark hair, was reading an English book. Yossi admired him so much because he could hold a conversation in German, Russian, Czech and Polish. He also admired that Mordecai could concentrate on reading even now as they hurtled towards the ground.

Tall blond-haired Leo was busy too. For most of the flight he had been trying to get at a spool of wire that was jammed down the side of the fuselage. Yossi knew that Leo would plan to use the wire or

trade it with someone. He was always on the lookout for any opportunity.

Now the plane lunged suddenly to the left and some of the children called out in fear. Yossi dragged himself to the window again to look out. Squinting in the bright light, he could see a range of mountains ahead, blue sparkling water beyond and miles and miles of green fields. They were out of the clouds.

Over England.

This was the place where they had been told they would be safe. A place where there would be no German soldiers and no concentration camps.

The only thing that Yossi knew about England was a distant memory of his father's bicycle. It was very special. So special that the tyres needed to be imported from another country. On the tyres – moulded into the rubber – were the words "MADE IN ENGLAND".

"What can you see out of the window?" Leo asked Yossi. "What does it look like?"

"I see Paradise," Yossi replied.

"Tell us more," Talia said. Talia was a young Polish woman who had come to take the children from a concentration camp in Europe to England and refuge. Yossi understood why she was asking. Talia wanted him to reassure this group of children who had spent the last six years terrified of what would happen to them next.

"It is beautiful," Yossi told the other children, turning to smile at them. "There are fields and roads and small villages. Just like back home in Poland ..."

Yossi stopped speaking once he saw some of the children frown at the mention of their homeland.

"But this is England," Yossi said quickly. "They're going to feed us. They're going to give us clothes. We'll be safe. Won't we, Talia?"

Talia nodded.

"What if it's not like that?" Mordecai asked Yossi quietly, once they were sat together again.

"It *will* be like that, Mordi." But Yossi's words were lost as the plane's engines began to roar ever louder and he felt a rush of fear.

The aeroplane was about to land.

Was England a nice place? *Would* it be safe?

"How do we know?" Mordecai asked again, his voice tense.

TWO

Yossi was not *really* sure that he and Mordecai would be safe when the plane finally landed in England. They had been lied to by the Nazis so many times about where they were going and what would happen next that it was impossible for him to truly feel safe. He reached into his pocket and touched the bar of chocolate that they had been given by the pilot before take-off and remembered the day it had all begun.

*

Yossi and his father had cycled into town to buy

bread and meat, as they did once a week for the special Sabbath meal they ate together as a family every Friday night. His mother and sisters – Mina and Anna – stayed at home to prepare the dining table, laying out the tablecloth and the silver candlesticks with the candles his mother would light before sunset.

The short shopping trip was one of the highlights of Yossi's week. It was a special time with his father, when he felt like he was one of the men. Yossi's dad would speak to friends in the square, share stories and have a drink in the cafe. And he would always buy Yossi a small bar of chocolate.

But everything was different that first Friday in September 1939. As he unwrapped the paper around the chocolate, Yossi noticed that the men were standing together in larger groups than normal. No one was smiling and some were talking in fast

agitated voices. Then a truck arrived and the driver stood on its bonnet and started shouting.

As Yossi tried to make out what the man was saying, his voice and all the other arguments were silenced by a droning noise. Distant at first, until, louder and louder, it became a roar. A single aeroplane was flying low over the town, following the long curve of the river, tipping slightly so that Yossi could see a black symbol on its side.

It was the first time he had seen the German cross.

The plane made a sharp turn, its engine screaming. Yossi's father grabbed him by the arm, told him to jump onto his bicycle and they raced home.

Yossi dropped his chocolate in the road.

It all happened so quickly. One moment a normal happy life, out with his father.

Then the German plane with its black cross.

Later that evening more aeroplanes came, like sudden storm clouds sweeping across the sky. These were larger. Bombers. The town square was attacked and dozens of buildings were destroyed as booms and cracks echoed off the valley sides. From his garden on the edge of the town, after the aeroplanes had gone, Yossi could smell burning and dust. It was like reading a story or a comic book about war, except it was real, happening to them. Now.

The next morning Yossi was woken by voices and clattering. Outside his bedroom window he saw a line of people leaving the village on foot, carrying suitcases, pushing carts, pulling animals on ropes behind them. One woman was clutching her Sabbath candlesticks to her chest as she passed by.

*

Now, coming in to land in England, Yossi shook his head. He didn't want these memories, these images, in his mind. He looked around and could see that Mordecai's eyes were still on him, searching for reassurance that they would be safe.

There were two things in Yossi's pocket. A spoon and the bar of chocolate. He took the bar of chocolate out of his pocket and showed it to his friend.

"What's this?" Yossi asked.

"Chocolate," answered Mordecai. "You've not eaten it?"

"I'm saving it," Yossi said. "But forget that. Listen to me. When were you last given chocolate before today?"

Mordecai hesitated. The plane was slowing down now. The engine roared, then there was a jolt as the wheels of the Stirling bomber bounced

twice on the runway, touching down to screams and shouts and bursts of laughter.

"Before the war," Mordecai replied at last.

"Exactly." Yossi tried to smile. "Life was good before the war, wasn't it?"

"Yes."

"We were given chocolate then?"

"Yes."

There was a final shudder as the Stirling bomber came to a stop.

"We have been given chocolate now," Yossi argued. "Things can be good again."

Mordecai nodded, then stared back at the pages of his book, leaving Yossi to continue wondering about what would really happen to them now they had reached England.

THREE

Once they had disembarked from the aeroplane, Yossi marvelled at the vast expanse of green grass on the airfield. He had lived in so many places over the last few years where there was no grass. Grass like this surprised him. It looked so green, so alive. He knelt on the ground and ran his fingers through the thick lush blades and smiled.

Then he heard the sound of an aeroplane.

Looking up, Yossi saw another Stirling bomber wobbling from side to side as it descended from the huge blue sky. He knew that there would be ten of

these aeroplanes arriving in total, each with thirty children on board.

Yossi stood and gazed around the airfield. A short walk away there was a small white building with a tower above it and a group of women standing beside a line of trestle tables. Two or three military trucks were parked behind them. Most of the children had already figured out that there was food and drink on the tables and were moving towards them. Yossi grabbed Mordecai and followed Leo in the direction of the food. Yossi noticed that Leo was holding the spool of wire he'd found on the plane.

Some of the women were among the children now, giving out white cups with small handles attached to the side.

"Tea?" a smiling woman asked him in English.

Yossi took the cup of tea. It looked pale. It had milk in it. "Thank you," he said.

The woman was about the same age as Yossi's mother when he'd last seen her. His eyes lingered on her face and she smiled back at him. Yossi turned away, not wanting to think about his mother. Not now. Not yet.

And there was their pilot, jumping down, exhausted, from the cockpit. He was tall, wearing a peaked cap and walking slowly in heavy boots towards the white building. His uniform troubled Yossi. Men in uniforms were usually cruel and dangerous. But Yossi wanted to speak to this man who had given him chocolate.

Yossi offered the pilot his cup and repeated the word the woman had used: "Tea?"

The pilot stopped. He looked confused but took the cup.

"Thank you," he said, and smiled as Talia joined them.

The pilot pointed at the plane. "You like aeroplanes?" he asked Yossi.

Talia translated for them.

"Yes," Yossi said. "When we saw you coming to bomb the Germans, we cheered. We would run out of our buildings in the concentration camp and watch you and hope that you'd drop bombs near where we were."

The pilot looked down at the ground and coughed. It was hard for Yossi to work out what he was thinking, but as he looked up, Yossi could tell he was having kind thoughts.

It was all in the eyes. Yossi understood that now. A man might have a uniform on, but you could tell if that man wanted to hurt you by looking in his eyes, not at his clothes.

What happened next astonished Yossi. The pilot took off his cap and – after brushing it down – handed it to him.

"For you," he said.

"Thank you," Yossi stuttered.

The pilot smiled and walked off towards the white building.

Yossi turned the cap over in his hands. Mordecai and Leo were with him now, Leo eyeing the hat as if it was a loaf of bread.

"It's mine." Yossi narrowed his eyes at Leo. "You can't take it. Do you understand?"

Leo tried to snatch the cap, laughing.

After cups of milky tea and hard biscuits, the children boarded a line of buses and trucks, each with thirty children and two adults aboard. As Yossi and his friends' truck moved off, Leo held open the flaps at the back, scouring the roadsides. From there, Yossi knew, Leo would keep watch. And Yossi was glad of it. Leo had always been like this: alert

to danger, working out what was coming next and being ready for it.

The story they had been told by Talia was that they would be staying in some hostels by a lake called Windermere. The hostels had been used by factory workers during the war. Hundreds of them had come to the area to build and fly special aeroplanes that could take off and land on the water of the lake. Huge seaplanes called Sunderlands.

Yossi trusted what Talia had told them. Well, he trusted her enough not to jump out of the truck and make a run for it. But they didn't know for sure where this truck was taking them. Was it *really* safe? Or was this just another trick to move them from one place to another without alarming them?

Yossi peered over Leo's shoulder, holding his pilot's cap on his head with both hands in case it blew away. At first all he could see was fields, their

stone walls casting late-evening shadows. But when the truck turned onto a wider road, they caught sight of the range of mountains to the west. The ones Yossi had seen from the aeroplane.

They made their way slowly through a town of small dark-stone houses. Yossi heard voices above the sound of the truck's engine, then saw a group of people standing outside a building that had an oil painting hanging above its door. The crowd were singing. They waved and lifted their glasses in the air as the children passed, seeming to toast them. Was this another sign they were going to be safe? Why would strangers wave to them if this was not a good country?

Yossi, Leo and some of the other children waved back. And – for a second – Yossi thought he saw his father among the crowd. Thin. Dark hair. Glasses. Smiling calmly back at them. Yossi leaned out,

desperate to see the man more closely. Could it be his father? Here? Yossi could hardly breathe; his heart was hammering. He tried to calm himself down.

The last time he had seen his father was seven months ago, when they were being marched from Auschwitz, just days before the Russians arrived to liberate it. But his father had disappeared during the march. Yossi was not sure what had happened to him.

It was possible he had just fallen back and been dealt with by the Germans. Or he could have escaped and joined one of the bands of partisan fighters that were attacking the Germans from the safety of the forests and mountains.

Yossi's father was not here in England: he knew that. But Yossi had to believe that his father was somewhere and that, one day soon, he would find him.

Their driver sounded his horn as the truck moved on, passing a small church with a square tower.

"I wonder if there's a synagogue?" Mordecai asked.

"Maybe," Yossi replied, happy to be distracted.

"But did they burn down the synagogues in England?"

"No." Yossi shook his head. "I don't think so."

"Mordecai," Talia interrupted. "At the estate where we will stay there is a Rabbi. And there will be a room to pray in, to hold religious services."

Yossi saw his friend smile.

The road led them between the steep hillsides of a valley, most of them covered in trees. Leo lifted the tarpaulin along the side of the truck and shouted, "LAKE!"

"Our lake?" Mordecai asked.

All of the children on the truck scrambled to the back to get a proper view, but Talia asked them to sit down.

"No," she told them. "This is not our lake. This one is called Ullswater. We are going to a place called the Calgarth Estate. Next to a lake called Windermere. Some of the families who live on the estate lost their homes when the Germans bombed the big cities here in England. There are also some workers from the seaplane factory still staying there with their families."

The truck moved slowly along the side of Lake Ullswater, the road winding to the contours of its shore. As darkness fell, Yossi and his friends stared through dark boughs and branches to the rippling water. They could see two bonfires burning on the far shore of the lake near a cluster of houses, the flames reflecting orange across the water.

"Why are there bonfires?" Mordecai asked Talia.

"They're celebrating the end of the war," Talia told them. "Today the war finally ended in Japan."

Ignoring the bonfires and their significance, Yossi peered at the lights coming from the houses, imagining what it would be like to be inside one of them with his mother and father and his sisters. He listened as Mordecai fired questions at Talia.

"What is Calgarth?" Mordecai asked.

"It's an estate of houses and buildings beside a lake. As I explained, families live there in the houses, but there are also hostels, blocks of bedrooms, where you will sleep. One little room each."

"Will there be beds?"

"Yes. In each room there is a bed, a table and a wardrobe."

"What sort of bed?"

"A mattress. Sheets. Blankets."

"Sheets?" Mordecai's voice was pitched high.

"Sheets."

"Will it be dark?" Mordecai gazed out of the truck at the night.

Yossi saw Talia look up and smile at him. "Each room has a light in the ceiling," she reassured him.

"An electric light? In each room?"

"Yes," Talia said. "You can leave your light on all night if you like. Light or dark: it's up to you. You won't be cold or hungry."

Then, after a pause, Mordecai asked, "Will there be guards?"

"No," Talia whispered, her eyes dropping from Yossi's gaze. "No guards."

FOUR

Yossi sat stiffly on the end of the bed.

His bed.

In his room.

It had been pitch-black when the buses and trucks finally pulled off the road onto the Calgarth Estate. The children could only see the shape of the buildings from electric lights shining through their windows.

On arrival, they had been stripped of their clothes and dusted with powder before being sent to have a shower. This had been *terrifying*. Yossi remembered how the Germans had disinfected them

with powder and taken their clothes and belongings from them when they arrived at the concentration camps. The echoes of the camps were hard to bear. But he still had his chocolate and was allowed to hold on to this and his pilot's hat and his spoon. And Talia was with them, insisting, again and again, that they were safe here, that this was England.

Next, they were given a vest, socks and some underpants to wear. Then, after they had been inspected by a doctor, they were led to their bedrooms.

The small room had white walls and blue curtains covering a window that looked out into complete darkness. All Yossi could see was a round face peering back at him. His own face, he knew. Though he didn't recognise himself. When he'd last seen his reflection properly, just after they were liberated and they found a mirror in one of the camp buildings, he'd been thin-faced, his skin grey in blue

and white striped clothing. Now his face had filled out and his hair had grown a little, having been shaved short for years.

There was a bed, a wardrobe and a small chest of drawers, just as Talia had promised. But Yossi had nothing to put in the wardrobe or drawers apart from his spoon and pilot's hat. There was a bunch of fresh flowers in a vase and a packet of sweets on the chest of drawers. The bed was soft and had blankets and white sheets, again like Talia had promised. Yossi had not seen or slept between sheets for several years. He ran his hand over the smooth clean surface and closed his eyes.

On the bed beside him was a canvas bag tied at the top with a piece of cord. He sat in silence, looking at the bag. In the room next door he could hear Leo repeatedly opening and closing his wardrobe doors, then some rattling. Hearing nothing from the room

to the other side, Yossi put his ear to the wall and listened to the low murmur of Mordecai singing or chanting. It was comforting to hear his two friends, to know they were next to him.

Leo, looking for things he could use.

Mordecai, praying. He was always praying.

There was an electric bulb in the ceiling above Yossi and a switch on the wall. He stood up to flick the switch on and off until he was shocked into stillness by the memory that he had once been in another room with a bed of his own, a wardrobe and his own electric light.

*

When he was at his most afraid at night in the concentration camps, Yossi had made up a game where he had to remember his bedroom at home.

In his mind, he would go around the room,

starting with the electric light switch by the door, recalling every picture on the wall, every piece of furniture. The wallpaper. The shape of the shelf of books – trying to remember the colour and the title on each spine. It would take time. He would try to do it in as much detail as he could, to make it feel like he was back there.

Sometimes it would help him fall asleep.

When the Germans had arrived in Yossi's village just days after the first bombing, they had forced his family out of their home and Yossi out of his bedroom, even though they were the fourth generation to have lived in that house. The Jewish families had to move to the centre of the town, where they were forced to share large buildings with only one room for each family. Sometimes one room for two families. This part of town had a wall built around it so that Jewish people could not leave.

Everyone called it the ghetto.

Yossi had later discovered that a Gentile – or non-Jewish – family with a son had moved into his home. Yossi knew the son. Tomasz. Yossi used to wonder if Tomasz had kept his books and pictures. If he played with the toys that Yossi was told not to bring when they had to leave their home quickly, taking only what they were able to carry.

Yossi and his father took their bicycles. They used them to help wheel what they could of their possessions into the ghetto: clothes, bedding, towels, crockery, cutlery.

And, like the lady who had walked past their house the day after the invasion, his mother had insisted that they bring the silver candlesticks for the Sabbath.

*

In the room at Calgarth, Yossi now pulled the cord loose at the top of the canvas bag and emptied its contents onto his bed. He found pyjamas. He checked for holes and stains, but they appeared to be new. They didn't look as if someone had died wearing them, so Yossi put them on.

He picked up the other objects. A toothbrush. A flannel. A bar of soap. Then, one by one, Yossi dropped them back in the bag before hiding it under the pillow along with his chocolate, sweets, the spoon he had brought with him and the pilot's hat he had been given, making sure they were all safe. Nobody could take anything from under his head as he slept without him knowing. He had learned this in the camps.

Standing for a few seconds, Yossi hesitated before he pulled back the white sheets and slipped into bed.

Even though the bed was so comfortable, sleep would not come.

At five-thirty the following morning, the sky above the Calgarth Estate began to change from black to deep blue, then pale blue, revealing a great expanse of forest and lake.

Windermere's water stretched out for miles. Unseen by human eyes, a large bird of prey skimmed across the ripples of the lake. A pair of deer stood quivering in the fields behind the six hostels where three hundred children lay in small rooms, some of them sleeping, some of them not.

Yossi's bed was empty.

Mordecai's too.

In Leo's room there were three boys in brand-new pyjamas curled around each other, head to toe, sleeping between crisp white sheets.

FIVE

And then it was morning. Their first day on the Calgarth Estate. Yossi, Leo and Mordecai stood shoulder to shoulder once they had left the safety of Leo's room and their hostel. For a while they were speechless. With wonder. It had been so dark when they arrived last night they had no idea, really, where they were. But now they could see what was to be their home for the next four or five months until winter came.

They were surrounded by lush green hills under a bright blue sky. There were huge clusters of trees, swallows flitting above them. They saw animals

grazing. To the north-west, mountains. They also saw people – mostly women and children – walking through the estate, gazing back to catch a glimpse of these boys who had arrived during the night.

But in spite of its beauty, the scene unsettled Yossi. He could feel his stomach turning with anxiety. They were living in new buildings made from red bricks; somewhere that had been built in the countryside, far away from towns and cities. This was like the places they'd been sent to before.

"Is it a camp?" Mordecai spoke, giving voice to Yossi's thoughts.

Leo shook his head. "No wire. No watchtowers. No—"

"—guards," Yossi finished for him.

Yossi nervously turned his spoon over and over in his hands, until he was distracted by a red van making its way along one of the roads on the estate.

He noticed other children had come from the hostels and were watching it too. When the van stopped, its driver, a young woman, climbed out and opened the back door of the vehicle. She pulled out a sack and a large brown package and carried them into one of the buildings.

A post woman, Yossi thought, and his heart leapt in his chest. Who would post letters to this place? Did anyone know they were here? Would there be letters for some of the children? Could there be a letter for him?

Talia had told him that the Red Cross were trying to reconnect people who had lost their families, separated by war and the concentration camps. People had escaped to every corner of Europe, even the United States. Was it too soon for Yossi to hope? To dream of being reunited with his father?

"Good boy," Yossi heard Leo say. And for a

moment he was confused. He turned to see that Leo
was feeding a small white dog.

"What are you giving it?" Yossi asked.

"Biscuits," Leo said. "From the airfield."

"What? To a dog?" Mordecai complained. "No
way. Give them to me."

Leo shook his head. "I want this dog to be a
friend to us."

"Why?"

"Dogs can be useful," Leo smirked, patting the
dog, then he stood up, aware that more children were
emerging from the long single-storey accommodation
blocks, lingering, unsure of what was going to happen
in the first hour of their first day in this new life.

Now Yossi saw his friend stiffen, his eyes
suddenly alert.

"We have to get over there now," Leo said,
giving up on the dog and pointing to a large building

in the centre of the estate. He walked away without waiting for a response. Yossi and Mordecai followed.

"Why?" Mordecai asked Leo, sounding as breathless as Yossi felt.

"The doors are opening," Leo said. "That's where they'll serve the food. I'm sure. It's going to be mayhem. Look. Those big lads are already at the door."

Leo was pointing at a group of tall boys.

"There will be enough for everyone," Yossi said, trying to distract his friend. "Talia told me so yesterday."

"Faster." Leo ignored him. "They might take it all."

Now that the doors of the building were open, there was a sudden change amongst the children. Rapid movement. Shouting, pushing. Adult voices trying to calm them.

Yossi felt sick. His heart was hammering with

the anxiety of it. It was always like this. At a new place you didn't know what was going to happen. You didn't know if you were going to get any food at all. He turned his spoon over in his hands as he followed Leo.

Yossi and Mordecai elbowed their way into a hall, walking tightly behind Leo. They only had seconds to make the right choice about where to sit.

Yossi wanted to believe what Talia had said. That there would be enough food for them all. That everyone would get a seat, that everyone would be fed. But there was more to it than that. There was *where* you sat, *who* you sat with, *where* the food was coming from.

The boys rapidly scanned the long tables, each intended to seat ten children on benches either side. They would have to be fast.

Light streamed in through high windows. Yossi

noticed what looked like serving hatches. A group of women in white aprons stood in front of the hatches watching them enter.

"Near there," Leo said, hitting Yossi on the shoulder. "The food comes from there."

Yossi nodded and led them towards the table nearest one of the hatches. They moved quickly. They weren't starving now, but ever since the war began food had been something you had to fight for, if there even was any. In the camps they had been given watery soup most days, where you only got a scrap of vegetable or meat if you were served towards the bottom of the container. Sometimes hard black bread.

Just as they were about to sit at the table near the hatch, a group of four of the big lads sat down and stared at Yossi, then Leo. Leo stood and eyed them, tipping his head back and holding the pose for a few seconds.

This was Leo being tough. This was Leo saying, *Don't mess with me and my friends*. Yossi liked that about Leo. He looked out for them.

But Leo wasn't looking for a fight today. He just wanted to be sure that they got fed. "Not near *them*. Move," he said. "We'll get nothing."

They sat at the hatch end of the next table and were joined quickly by seven others. The tables were laid with white tablecloths and plates. Yossi was shocked to see a plate. He'd eaten out of a cracked bowl or from his hands for the last five years. He'd forgotten plates existed.

He then spotted the cutlery and quickly pocketed his own spoon. He wouldn't need it today.

And then they waited. Watching.

As they waited, Yossi felt as if every one of his muscles had been pulled tight. His stomach ached. His brain was overheating. What if they got nothing?

What if they missed this meal? When was the next one? If he got anything, what should he do with it? Eat a bit, hide the rest? Take it and eat it all now, so no one could steal it? Question after question ripped his thoughts to pieces. He hated feeling like this.

Yossi's thoughts were interrupted by the movement of women in aprons around them. They passed baskets of something white down the tables, along with glass jars containing something red.

"It's cake," Leo gasped. "Can you believe that they eat cake for breakfast?"

"And jam," Mordecai added.

It was hard to sit still and watch other tables being served first. Yossi was craning his neck to see. *Would* there be enough?

"Is it real?" he asked Mordecai, breathless. "The jam?"

Mordecai shrugged.

Then a tall lady with curly hair stuffed into a net on her head put a large basket and two jars of jam in front of them.

"Morning, boys," she said. "I'm Marion. Some bread and jam for you."

"Thank you," Mordecai said, then translated "bread" and "jam" to Yossi and Leo.

"Thank you," the other two echoed.

"Bread?" Leo asked when the woman had gone. He took the three largest pieces and put them on his, Yossi and Mordecai's plates. Then, as Yossi and Mordecai stuffed bread in their vests, Leo slipped one of the jars of jam onto his lap. "This is bread?" he asked again.

"It's cake," Yossi said, taking three more pieces for himself and his friends.

The food in front of them was white and soft. They were used to dark bread, solid, made of rye. Even before the war they had never seen white bread.

"She said bread," Mordecai shouted, frustrated. "I know the word for bread and she said bread."

"Put the jam back," Yossi said to Leo, aware the other children on the table were already on their feet, their mouths open in protest.

Leo smiled and returned the jam.

Yossi didn't miss the fact that Mordecai closed his eyes and lowered his head over his food before he ate.

In a quiet corner, away from the door, younger children were eating with adults. Some of the little ones looked nervous, flinching from the older children as if they were wild animals. The younger children were always like that. They'd lived most, if not all, of their lives in concentration camps. They probably had no memory of their mother or father. Or what a mother or father even was.

Yossi shuddered.

There was no talking now as the children ate, tearing at the bread with their hands, dipping it in dollops of jam they'd spooned onto their plates or straight into the jar. Yossi could hear chewing, jars being scraped out by spoons. As he ate, he felt the food flooding his body with warmth and energy.

Another basket of bread arrived.

Another jar of jam.

Then, suddenly, there was shouting, the noise of a bench scraping on the floor. The three friends turned around to see that a fight had broken out on the next table.

"What is it?" Yossi asked.

"Those taller lads – Heinrich and Thomas," Leo grinned, the white of the bread showing through the gaps in his teeth. "They're fighting each other over the food."

As the pushing and shoving continued, Yossi

took the chance to stuff another hunk of bread into his trouser pocket and noticed Leo and Mordecai do the same.

"There is plenty to go around." Talia addressed the next table, her voice loud and hard. "Stop this at once. No more fighting."

The fighting stopped. Immediately. No one had heard Talia raise her voice before.

"I will shout more if I have to," Talia went on. "I don't want to, but I will. There is enough food for today and for tomorrow and after that. Anyone who wants to see is very welcome to come and look in the kitchens."

Leo was on his feet, his chair clattering behind him onto the stone floor. "Come on," he said.

Yossi shook his head. His friend was impossible, desperate to get into the kitchens. Yossi knew he'd be thinking of what he could find, what he could use.

"I mean it," Leo insisted. "Come on. Now."

Leo and Yossi joined some of the other boys in the kitchen. It was a space half the size of the dining hall, with large ovens and tables to prepare food. There were heaps of white bread loaves stacked on one table. The boys were introduced to a tall dark-haired lady.

"Dorothy is in charge of the kitchen," Talia told them.

"Where's Mordecai?" Leo asked Yossi, looking around.

Yossi shrugged.

"And in here," Dorothy said, translated by Talia, "we have supplies for meals for a week, a month. You don't have to worry, boys. We have food for as long as you need it."

Then Talia added quietly, "You won't go hungry again. I promise."

The boys fell silent as they stared at a large

room stacked with bags of flour, oil, crates of vegetables, cheeses. Yossi inhaled. The smells coming off the food were dizzying.

On the cookers three giant pans of soup were boiling. Peelings of chopped onions and carrots lay on the kitchen top. Yossi wanted to ask what would happen to the peelings. He was anxious that they'd be thrown away and wasted. He was about to say something, but the stunned silence was broken not by him but by Mordecai carrying in several empty plates and pieces of cutlery from their table in the hall, clinking and clattering as he stumbled.

Dorothy helped Mordecai put the plates down, then she spoke to him kindly in English. None of the other boys understood what she'd said, but Talia smiled when she heard. Yossi took the opportunity, in the confusion, to grab a handful of carrot peelings and stuff them into his clothes.

Now Mordecai hung his head and stepped away. He stared hard at the floor, silent.

"What did the lady say to you?" Yossi asked him.

Mordecai shook his head.

Talia explained. "She said that he is good to clear the table after a meal. That his mother would be very proud of him."

Mordecai kept his eyes on the floor of the kitchen so that he didn't have to explain that his mother would not be proud. That she was dead.

SIX

Several days after the children had arrived at
Windermere, there were still not enough clothes
for them all to wear. They had underpants, vests
and socks, but some had nothing to put over them.
Despite this, Yossi had settled into feeling safe.
His fears that the place would turn out to be a
concentration camp were fading. He sometimes saw
men in heavy boots and overalls covered in oil. They
scared him, so he avoided them, even though he had
been told that they were workers from the seaplane
factory and were no threat.

Today, the children stood in doorways, sheltering

from the fine rain that was drifting low between the mountains; a gentle but warm breeze blew across the estate.

Yossi had spotted two bicycles propped against a wall opposite, but his attention was distracted by the sight of Leo talking to the larger boys who always sat on the next table at breakfast. Leo took something out of his pocket. The boy did the same. A short conversation, then an exchange and Leo was striding back to Yossi and Mordecai.

"I knew he loved chocolate," Leo explained.

"Eh?"

"That Heinrich ... whatever his name is. Don't you remember how he went mad for the chocolate the pilot gave us?" Leo held up a jar of jam. "I saw him swipe this at breakfast today. I knew he'd trade it for a bar of chocolate. I reckon he'd have swapped it for a *piece* of chocolate."

"And what are you going to do with the jam?" Yossi asked.

"Something," Leo grinned. "I don't know yet."

Yossi laughed and looked longingly at the two bicycles again.

When had he last ridden a bike?

A long time ago.

*

Yossi would never forget seeing the poster in the main square of the ghetto, where the Germans often put up signs telling Jews what they could and could not do.

He remembered not being allowed to sit on benches in the park.

Having to walk not on the pavements but in the gutter.

Having to sew a yellow star on his clothes.

The new rule that day was:

**All Jews are to hand over their
bicycles to the authorities.
Adults and children must comply.**

Yossi and his father had spent some time looking over their bicycles one last time before they gave them up. They brushed the brake pads. Wiped down their frames. Cleaned the chains. Then they walked their bicycles through the narrow streets to the square in the centre of the ghetto.

On the way, his father made Yossi cross the road. At first he wasn't aware why. Then he saw. Three German soldiers were laughing. And on the ground, kneeling in the gutter, was a Jewish man with a black hat and a long beard. The soldiers were pulling hard at the man's beard. It was difficult

to hear the sound of the man crying out in pain because of the laughter of the soldiers.

"Dad?" Yossi asked.

"Yes, Yossi," his father replied.

"Why do we let them do that to him? Why don't we help? And why must we just hand our bicycles over to the soldiers?"

Yossi would never forget what happened next. The memory would influence all his decisions about what to do or how to act over the following six years. They watched as an older woman went over to challenge the soldiers who were abusing the bearded man. Two of the soldiers turned on her. One of them pushed her over as the other took his rifle, held it at hip-height and fired a bullet into her chest.

Neither Yossi nor his father said anything more as they approached the group of soldiers who were collecting bicycles. Yossi could not speak. All he could do was walk to the soldier, hand his bicycle over, look at the floor, then move away.

He did notice that the Germans smiled at each other, looking pleased because Yossi and his dad's bicycles were in very good condition.

Yossi had mixed feelings about this reaction of the German soldiers. He was *angry* because he was handing over his bicycle, the thing that had given him the freedom to explore the streets and lanes of where he once lived. But he was *proud* too, because the Germans would now know that a Jew could have a good bicycle and keep it in such excellent condition.

Walking away, his father waited until they were out of earshot of the soldiers, then he whispered, "One day you will ride a bicycle again. I promise you."

Yossi's father didn't mention the man with the beard or the woman who had gone to help him.

*

Now Yossi looked at his two friends standing in the doorway, sheltering from the fine rain. That sudden memory of his bicycle being taken had allowed a flood of other images in. Things he didn't want to remember.

Yossi rubbed his face. He tried to fix on what his father had said to him: that one day he would ride a bicycle again. Today was the day that promise from his father could come true, even if his father wasn't here to share the experience.

"Come on," Yossi urged. "The bicycles."

"Don't we need proper clothes?" Mordecai complained.

"Why?" Yossi asked.

"We can't go out in underwear," Mordecai insisted. "It's raining."

"It's warm rain," Yossi said, stepping out into it. "It's nice."

No reply.

Yossi eyed the two bicycles again, then walked into the rain. If he didn't do this, someone else would.

"Yossi?" Leo called out after him. "What's going on?"

"I want to ride a bicycle," Yossi shouted.

And now, as he heard his friends coming after him, Yossi climbed onto one of the bicycles. He smiled. It felt good.

His two friends shared the other bicycle, Leo at the front. Mordecai on the back. Then the three of them were wheeling wildly round the Calgarth Estate, stones crunching under their tyres as Yossi recovered his ability to balance, then pedal hard. The tyres skidded as he accelerated, the wind in his ears,

the rain on his face, Leo and Mordecai laughing and calling out behind him. And for a few seconds, Yossi closed his eyes as he sped along, just like he used to, the grin spreading across his face.

SEVEN

Having cycled round the estate, the boys found their way to the lake. Windermere was a huge expanse of water stretching for what seemed like miles in each direction. The sun had come out again and was sparkling off the surface.

Yossi lay on his back, his hands behind his head, staring at swallows flitting down to catch flies above the surface of the water. He remembered birds behaving this way at the lake where he used to go on holiday with his parents and sisters.

Behind him, Mordecai was trying to read an English newspaper called the *Westmorland Gazette*

that he had picked up during their first days at Calgarth, and Leo was working on the bicycle he'd been riding. He'd discovered that the brakes were broken. Using the spool of wire he'd found on the Stirling bomber, he had managed to fix them. Now he was testing the brakes and whistling to himself.

Yossi's attention skipped from the lake to a buzzard that was hovering high over a field away from the shore. Again, he felt a rush of pleasure at being by this lake.

"Do you remember," he asked, his mind on swallows and buzzards, "there were no birds? I have missed birds."

"Where were there no birds?" Mordecai asked.

"There," Yossi said. "In the camps. There were no plants, no trees, no grass, so why would birds come? We had eaten all the plants and grass ..."

The silence that met Yossi's question made him

recoil. Leo continued to work on his bicycle. Mordecai stared at his newspaper. And Yossi knew he had to change the subject. Why would his friends want to talk about that? Why would he?

"What's it about?" he asked Mordecai quickly. "The thing you are reading?"

Mordecai rustled his newspaper.

"The people we saw who were singing in the town we drove through when we arrived," Mordecai said. "And the bonfires. Do you remember? Look here. They were celebrating. Talia was right."

Yossi remembered the groups of people raising their glasses to the truck as it passed by. And the bonfires at the lake's side.

He looked at the newspaper. Mordecai translated for him:

PEACE ON EARTH

JAPAN SURRENDERS: WORLD WAR 2 ENDS

"The war really is over," Mordecai said. "Everywhere. For everyone."

And then, before he could answer, Leo was thrown onto his back.

The attack came from nowhere. A small dog was on top of him – the same dog he'd fed biscuits to days earlier. Leo laughed and wrestled it gently to the ground, then took a piece of bread from his bag and gave it to the dog as it growled and raced between the boys, touching them each playfully with its wet black nose.

After the commotion, Yossi saw that the dog was not alone.

"Leo?" he said.

"What?"

"There's a girl."

The three boys looked away from the shore, back into the woodland that separated the Calgarth Estate from the lake. A girl aged about eight with light curly hair stood there, a rope dangling at her side.

"Maybe it's her dog?" Mordecai suggested.

"Ask her," Leo whispered.

Mordecai blushed. "Why me?"

"Because she's probably not that good at speaking Polish," Leo growled.

Mordecai frowned. "Is your dog this?" he asked the girl in unsteady English.

The girl smiled and nodded. Then she pointed at the bicycle and said something else in English.

Mordecai translated. "It's her father's bicycle. Leo, you have to take it back."

"Do I?" Leo grumbled.

Yossi stood up. "You do," he said firmly.

"But I mended it."

"I'm sure they'll be very grateful," Yossi said.

Leo smiled and the three boys walked towards the girl, the dog staying close to Leo's heel.

The girl's home was in the middle of a row of houses on the far side of a large playing field at the centre of the Calgarth Estate. One storey of red brick with a slate roof and a chimney. There was a wooden trellis running up either side of the front door, white roses climbing there.

A woman was standing looking out of an open window, a cloth hanging down from her hand as she watched three older boys accompany her little girl and dog home.

She came to the front door to meet them. There

was a smell of cooking wafting from the house. Yossi recognised her as one of the women who worked in the estate kitchen. He wished he could remember her name.

Yossi noticed tomato plants growing on the insides of the windows. The sharp scent of the plants shook him. His mother used to grow tomatoes. On the table was a large wooden radio with a white and red dial at the centre. He'd had one of those at home too. He hadn't thought about it for six years. The memory shocked him.

"Ah ... you've found Dad's bicycle," the woman said, joined by a second woman who was alongside her now. "And Spot," she said, naming the dog. "Where's he been all morning?"

Mordecai translated for Yossi and Leo.

"Sorry, bicycles," Leo said quickly. In English.

The woman smiled. Mordecai patted his friend

on the back, impressed that Leo had picked up so much English in just one week.

"We are Mordecai, Yossi and Leo," he told her.

"I'm Dorothy," the woman said. "Hello again. And welcome. This is Joan, my sister. And your new friend, my daughter, is Joyce," she added, ruffling the girl's hair.

Leo put his hand into his bag, causing the dog to sit obediently and stare into his eyes. Leo took out his jar of jam and gave it to Dorothy.

Yossi noticed her frown, confused at first. She would know this jam was from the estate kitchen.

"Jam?" She stifled a laugh.

"Jam," Leo said seriously.

Then she spoke to Mordecai. "How do I say thank you?" she asked. "In your language?"

"*Dziekuje*," Mordecai told her.

"*Dziekuje*," Dorothy said to Leo.

Leo bowed, then looked in through the door.

"That smells good," he said in Polish.

Mordecai reluctantly translated – he knew what his friend was up to.

"Would you like some?" Dorothy asked. "It's scouse. Like stew. Just vegetables, no meat. With bread?"

Mordecai explained what she had said and all three boys nodded, stepping forward at once.

They sat at a heavy wooden table, large brown bowls in front of them steaming with vegetable stew. There was a photograph of a very young man on the mantelpiece above the fire. His face looked a bit like Dorothy's. Yossi wondered if he was her son, and whether he was dead or alive. He decided not to ask.

Seeing Dorothy watching him, Yossi pointed at the radio.

"Radio?" he asked.

Dorothy smiled kindly. And then Joyce was talking excitedly.

"Yes. It is. It's new. We used it to listen to Mr Churchill on VE Day."

"VE Day?" Mordecai asked.

"Victory in Europe Day. When the Germans surrendered," Joyce chattered on, looking at her mum for approval. "Then we had a party. There was tea and cakes. We had long tables outside and Mummy made bunting."

"What is bunting?" Mordecai asked.

"Little flags. Red, white and blue," Joyce enthused. "And Mr Churchill said: 'In all our long history, we have never seen a greater day than this.' And everyone was laughing, then crying, then laughing again."

"Do you remember that day, boys?" Dorothy asked, putting her hand on Joyce's head.

"Yes," Mordecai said. "This is the day we were free."

Dorothy then gave them knives and spoons, but these were ignored as the boys ate with their hands, using the bread to scoop and soak up the stew. All this was done in silence. Joyce sat watching, then began eating with her hands too, grinning wildly.

They continued eating. Yossi occasionally caught Dorothy and Joan studying them, both with a look in their eyes that Yossi had seen before.

*

After a few weeks in the ghetto, people were starving. Yossi and his family had brought a little food with them but not much. They had traded some of their possessions and spent most of their savings.

But there was not always time to find food, to trade, to do jobs to earn food or even money. Because Yossi and his father were required to work.

The Germans had everyone's name on a list. Men and boys over the age of ten had to work in the factory just outside the ghetto, making uniforms. They all knew who the uniforms were for and why. They were for German soldiers to wear in cold weather. Germany was at war with Russia now, too. They would need thick clothes to stay alive. Yossi and his father had to make those clothes. Or be shot.

They were not paid to work. They were forced. Slaves. Every morning, they reported to the main square of the ghetto, in the shadow of a Catholic church, from where they were marched to the factory.

It was the look in Dorothy's eyes that had brought back the memory.

The memory of the non-Jewish women who

70

worked alongside Yossi and his father in the factory.
The women were given food at lunchtime and had
breaks to rest. Yossi's father said that they were
paid, that they weren't slaves.

When the women came back from their
lunch-time break, they would, if there were no guards
nearby, occasionally slip a slice of bread underneath
the machine Yossi was working at. Sometimes
buttered. Other times they would bring whole bags
full of potato peelings from home and leave them for
him. They could see that Yossi was slowly starving.

Yossi remembered being desperate to eat the
slice of bread or the potato peelings as he worked in
the freezing cold of the factory. But he never did. His
sisters and his mother needed the food just as much
as him. At the end of the day he would hide the
scraps under his clothes and take them back to their
room in the ghetto.

Yossi knew that there was a good chance he would be dead if those kind women had not helped him.

*

Yossi was jolted out of his memories when a man appeared in the doorway of Dorothy's house. He was tall and had black smears on his face and hands. He wore overalls. For a second the three boys stared at the man, then they all stood slowly, holding their breath, expecting the worst. This was the man whose bicycle they had taken.

"I hope you boys have left some for me," the man said. He frowned, staring at the pan, then his face changed into a warm smile as he sat and ladled some stew into his bowl. "Only kidding, boys. You're very welcome here."

"This is Arthur," Dorothy explained. "My husband. He works at the seaplane factory, over there."

Mordecai translated. Arthur was one of the men who had built the seaplanes they had heard of – ones that Yossi longed to see in action. These huge flying boats had been built and tested on the lake here, then used to help Britain and its allies defeat the Nazis.

For Yossi it was hard enough to believe that planes could take off from solid ground, never mind from water, and he wished he could ask the man about them and how they worked. But he knew that even Mordecai could not translate a conversation like that.

Later, after they had thanked the family and were heading back to their rooms, Mordecai told Leo and Yossi about what had been said.

"That family are not from here. Windermere. They are from a city called Liverpool. Their house was bombed by the Nazis. They had no home. They moved here after that."

Yossi swallowed.

"The picture of the young man. Is that Dorothy and Arthur's son?"

Mordecai nodded. "Yes. They told me his name is Peter."

"Is he dead?" Leo said.

"No." Mordecai shook his head. "I don't think so ... well, he was fighting. Near Japan, they said. But they've not heard from him for months. But I think they are worried that they will never hear from him again."

Yossi rubbed his face. He thought about how Dorothy and her husband must feel not knowing where their son was. Then he thought about his own father.

Yossi was still confused about how they had been separated. The Nazis had been marching them from one concentration camp – Auschwitz – to another. Or from a train? He couldn't remember.

Yossi had been unwell, falling behind. His father was still with him, but then suddenly he wasn't. Yossi remembered Mordecai and Leo helping him as he was so weak. They were all so exhausted and frightened. One minute his father was there and the next he was gone.

He'd just disappeared.

EIGHT

It was late August and the children had been at Windermere for two weeks when a sleek black car eased slowly onto the Calgarth Estate.

It had become a kind of game for the children now: waiting for vehicles to turn in from the main road. Who was inside? What did they want? Was something about to change?

Yossi imagined all of them were thinking what he was thinking. That it could be, might be, a father, a mother, a brother: someone coming to find them.

They all longed to be found.

The children had been sitting around on the

grass. There was a low hubbub of voices, dozens of conversations. But all eyes were now on the sleek black car. It looked like the car of someone important. Yossi noticed some of the boys quietly getting to their feet and moving into the hostel and their rooms. He felt the same impulse: that fear of important men, the kind of men who decided what would happen to you next.

Once the car stopped, a man emerged. Yossi was certain he could smell perfume or something, even from where they sat, nearly fifty metres away. The man was tall and smartly dressed. His eyes searched the groups of the boys as if he was desperately looking for someone.

Yossi felt sure he was thinking what everyone else was thinking. *Is that my father? It could be. I've not seen him for months. I can't remember even what he looks like. What if he has come for me?*

Yossi watched Talia approaching the man, some papers in her hands. Next to her, a boy: Felix. He had on a shirt and short trousers.

Yossi felt as if his heart had stopped. He could barely breathe.

All conversations were silenced now. It was so quiet that Yossi could hear Felix's quick footsteps as he ran towards the man.

"His father," Mordecai croaked.

The three boys and dozens of others watched from the grass and from windows as the man knelt down and embraced his son and shook hands with Talia.

Then – after chatting and laughing – father and son were climbing into the black car. And the black car was moving away, leaving Talia waving after them.

Yossi, Mordecai and Leo did not speak. Nor did

they look at each other. They had seen the look on Felix's face: his smile, his tears.

Now Yossi imagined another car coming down the road. But he could only imagine as far as the car stopping. Not the door opening. Not running into his father's arms. It was too much for Yossi to dare to dream. That his father might show up here.

Tomorrow.

Next week.

Never.

NINE

A few days after Felix had left, Yossi, Leo and Mordecai had their first lesson outside under one of the great beech trees on the edge of the estate. Ten of them sat at a large wooden table, all wearing the clothes that had now arrived.

One of the many things Jewish children like Yossi had been deprived of when the Nazis came was school. Now Yossi was safe and no longer starving to death, he would have chosen a lesson like this over a meal if he had to.

He was desperate to know what was inside the exercise books the children attending earlier

lessons had been given: so many of them seemed to be clutching and scribbling in these books as if they were their most prized possessions.

But his was empty.

"What's in your notebook?" Yossi asked Leo, leaning over to look.

Leo flicked through. "Nothing."

Yossi was confused. He didn't understand. But then one of the adults arrived. Yossi had seen her around but not spoken to her. She was usually with the younger children as they ate their meals and she worked in the block where there were art supplies for drawing and painting.

Marie Paneth introduced herself. She was Austrian and a Jew. Like Talia, she had come to England before the war. She would teach them English.

Over the next hour, they learned several words or very short phrases:

Hello.

Goodbye.

Thank you.

My name is …

I was born in …

It was thrilling to be learning again. Yossi knew Mordecai would be excited about it. But he was surprised to see how engaged Leo was. He always thought Leo would be one of those boys who messed around and skipped school whenever he could. So once Marie stopped teaching and was looking at a piece of paper, he quizzed his friend.

"How was it for you?"

Leo smiled politely and bowed to Yossi.

"Hello. My name is Leo, thank you. I was born in Poland. Goodbye."

Yossi laughed.

Then Leo switched to speaking in Polish. "I like lessons. At my school we had a table outside under a tree, just like this. Miss Boniek would teach us writing."

"Our school was on a busy road," Mordecai said. "No garden. We had to work inside. It was dark and cold."

Now Leo and Mordecai looked at Yossi, expecting some sort of school memory from him. But the only thing he could recall was the day he showed up to school only to find another German sign:

Jewish children are no longer allowed to attend school.

This is due to overcrowding.

His mother led him away quickly, through his old school friends, holding his hand so hard it hurt, even though Yossi was telling her that his class wasn't

overcrowded, that there were only seven of them, that it must be a mistake.

Yossi didn't want to speak about that to Leo and Mordecai.

Then more memories came back, taking him by surprise. An image flashed into his mind of the tutor who had taught Yossi secretly in the ghetto. A young man who could only just have been out of school himself. He was called Nathaniel. He had exceptionally dark hair and wore his glasses on the end of his nose like an old man. Yossi felt a sharp pain in his stomach and in his head: he didn't want to think about Nathaniel either.

Fortunately he was distracted from his thoughts by Marie, who had more to say before they were dismissed.

"I need to speak to you about the exercise books I have given you," she said.

Yossi sat up, his attention fully on his teacher now.

"In a few days," Marie went on, "we will be visited by the Red Cross."

Yossi shifted in his seat and glanced at his two friends. After they were liberated by the Russians in the Theresienstadt concentration camp, it was the Red Cross who came to take care of them, brought them food, made them safe. Now the Red Cross were coming to help them again. That was good.

"They want to take details," Marie went on, "lists of the names of your families, to try to reunite people ... people like yourselves who have become split up from loved ones because of the war."

Marie paused, expecting questions, but none of the children spoke.

Yossi glanced at Leo and Mordecai. Both knew they had no parents or siblings to find. But there

could be aunts, cousins. There was still some hope.

"You all have your notebooks and pencils now," Marie went on. "Over the next few days please try to make a list of the names of your family. Parents. Siblings. Grandparents. Aunts. Uncles. Cousins. Anyone you remember from family gatherings, bar mitzvahs, weddings. Try to remember where they lived, their jobs. When did you lose touch with them? The more information you can provide the better. Do you understand? And, of course," Marie paused again, "if you know they did not survive. If you know that ... then don't include their name."

Yossi understood. He opened his notebook and wrote the name David Frenkle, 44, father. He kept his pencil poised over the page. Then he wrote the names of his mother, Rebecca Frenkle; Anna Frenkle and Mina Frenkle, his sisters; his four grandparents; his aunts; uncles; all seventeen of his cousins. Some

of his cousins had children. He wrote their names down too.

Around him it was quiet. But Yossi didn't look up. Now he took his pencil and began to cross names out.

His mother's parents. He had learned they were dead quite soon after the Germans invaded. His father's mother died a normal death before the war. His father's father? He didn't want to think about that, but Yossi knew he was dead.

Then more names. Cousins and uncles that he knew were dead. He crossed out several, each time pausing over their name before drawing a line through it slowly, memories of that person coming to him, then fading.

When Yossi looked up, he saw that no one else had left the wooden table under the tree. They were all writing or staring at pages with lists of names.

Some of the children could not write the names of their family for themselves and were being helped by adults.

Yossi finished by crossing his mother's name out. Then those of his sisters, Anna and Mina. But his father's name was still there. He drew a circle around it.

TEN

It was dinner time when they'd finished writing and crossing out the names of their families. Yossi felt so exhausted he could hardly lift himself off the benches under the beech tree.

The doors to the dining hall had opened. A gust of wind ruffled across the lake and up through the trees, bringing a coolness to the air. The light was fading sooner in the evenings now. Autumn was coming. Like it came in the camps, bringing darkness and cold – brutal cold.

They did not rush into the dining hall any more. Within a few days of arriving, the children

had secured their own places on their own benches. Yossi, Leo and Mordecai were near the front of the hall and were always joined by a group of seven younger boys. Marion or Dorothy would deliver the food to Leo at the top of the table. Leo would pass it down, making sure everyone got what they wanted. Very few of them hoarded bread or stole peelings now. They had discovered that the bread would quickly go mouldy if they hid it in their wardrobe or under their mattress. But fruit and sugar still remained fair game.

The boys at Yossi's table had become used to using a knife and fork again instead of their hands. They had taught themselves to eat slowly without fear that food would be taken away or stolen by the person next to them.

Yossi enjoyed eating with a knife and fork. This was something else they had had taken from them

by the Nazis: eating at a table in a civilised way, like humans, not animals. It was almost as if the Nazis had wanted to turn them into animals. *Maybe it made it easier for them to do what they did to us*, he thought.

Because there was always cutlery for them to use, Yossi didn't need to keep his spoon with him all the time now. Until recently he had. There was a hole in the lining of his shirt where he'd kept it. Then – when he was sleeping – he'd put his hand around it. His spoon had been his only possession in the camps. But you could lose a spoon, have it taken away. Then you had to hunt for another. He had taken the one he had now from the lining of the shirt of a dead man. He wasn't proud of that, but he wasn't ashamed either. The dead man would have done the same if it were the other way round.

Yossi shuddered and turned his thoughts away

from the concentration camps to today. To now. He was happy that he knew he could leave cutlery to be washed for the next meal, not steal it. There would be food the next day. And cutlery.

In the dining hall today there was a sharp and familiar smell in the air. Something new.

Tomato soup.

And another thing was different: a large group of people from the estate stood in the doorway watching as the women served each child with a bowl of soup. Yossi had seen some of them while they had been in their lesson. They had been carrying baskets and bowls full of tomatoes from their homes to the kitchens. Now it all made sense to him.

Mordecai, to Yossi's left, was saying a prayer over his food. He was not the only one. Several other children were doing the same. There was a low calm murmur of voices as their soup was served.

As he listened to Mordecai pray, Yossi watched steam rising from his bowl. The smell was intoxicating, like the soup his mother used to make. He could smell basil too. He remembered basil. If his mother was cooking, she would send Yossi into the garden to pick some basil, or some other herb, from one of the pots. He remembered the smell of the herbs on his fingers after he'd taken them to her.

Dorothy spoke to the children in a clear voice. "Before you eat," she said, "you should know that the families on the estate have provided the main ingredient for this meal."

The low hubbub of boys' voices was silenced as Talia translated Dorothy's words.

"Tomatoes are a struggle to come by at the moment, but the locals have brought you theirs. Some bought them using their ration books. Others grew their own. They bring them as a gift to you."

Yossi heard voices of complaint. Then Mordecai was on his feet. "It's their tomatoes," he said. "They grew them. They should eat the soup. Their families should eat the soup. They have children who need to eat tomatoes too."

All the children had put their spoons down.

Yossi saw Talia translating for the local people, who began to shake their heads, then speak to her.

Talia addressed the dining hall now. "They want you to have their tomatoes to show to you that you are part of the Calgarth Estate," she said. "They want you to be strong and healthy. You should eat the soup and enjoy it. The happier you look eating it, the more pleased they will be."

Talia had spoken in Polish. Nobody translated what she had said back into English.

The children ate. They didn't need to pretend to enjoy the soup: it was delicious. To Yossi it felt

like his veins were running with warmer blood.
He smiled as he ate. He liked these people of the
Calgarth Estate. They were kind.

He was overwhelmed to remember that people
could be kind.

Yossi went to bed feeling stronger after they had
eaten the tomato soup.

The boys slept alone now, most nights. They
enjoyed having a bed to themselves, the clean white
sheets. And Yossi liked to be away from Mordecai
at night because he sometimes flailed about as if
he was fighting the bed clothes that had wrapped
around his legs. And away from Leo, too, who snored,
sometimes sounding like one of the cows on the
hillsides around them.

Alone in his bed, Yossi re-lived the memories
of his mother that the soup had brought back to

him. He thought, too, about the English lesson he'd enjoyed that day. But in the dark, with the light off, those memories soon faded and his mind turned again to his dark-haired bespectacled young tutor, Nathaniel. The one he was trying desperately *not* to remember.

Yossi opened his eyes to stop the scene that was replaying itself in his mind. But it was hopeless. The memories came whether he wanted them or not.

*

After Yossi's family had been forced out of their home to live in the ghetto and he and his sisters were prevented from going to school, his parents still wanted them to learn. All the Jewish families wanted their children to have an education, however bleak their lives were. So after he finished his shift in the factory, Yossi joined other boys and girls

for a lesson with Nathaniel. In secret. If they were discovered, they would be punished. Severely.

They'd been studying the Bible that last day. Yossi had read out a section and Nathaniel was asking him what it meant when the door burst open. He would never forget that moment, just as he would never forget the SS insignia on the soldiers' shoulders.

The violence – even though it did not touch Yossi or any of his secret classmates that day – was appalling.

The soldiers could do anything. And they did.

One of them grabbed Nathaniel by his jacket and hauled him out into the street, bouncing him down the stone steps. The other soldier grabbed an armful of books and glared at the children cowering there. For a second Yossi thought they would be dragged out too. But the soldier just took the school books and walked out.

Yossi stood at the window and watched Nathaniel being punched, then having his legs kicked from under him. Bending low, one of the SS men repeatedly struck Nathaniel on his head and upper body with the butt of his rifle before he was bundled into the back of a truck. The soldiers were rough with him, even though he put up no resistance. Then the truck moved off and all that was left was the sharp smell of its exhaust fumes floating through the window, a large smear of blood on the cobbles outside and the empty table where the school books had once been.

That was the last time Yossi had been in a classroom before today.

ELEVEN

A few days later the children were playing a British game called rounders in the central grassy area of the estate when a bus eased off the main road. It was a month after they had arrived in England.

Jock Lawrence was a sports teacher who had come in to work with the children, to build their fitness and strength. He was now explaining the rules and showing them how to hit the small hard ball with a bat, then run from base to base without being struck out. The weather was clear and sunny, but some of the boys were wearing their jackets for the first time because of the cooler autumn air.

The boys loved Lawrence. He was tall and strong. He wore sports clothes and running vests. He was never out of breath like they often were.

Leo was the first to spot the bus. He had been waving to Joyce, who was walking with her dog and some other local children, when his attention moved to the road. He pointed the vehicle out to the others and the game stopped.

Yossi studied the bus, trying to peer in through the windows. He didn't see children. The figures coming off the bus were adult men, smartly dressed. The Calgarth Rabbi was there to greet them, wearing his robes. He shook each man's hand firmly as the boys looked on.

The men were dressed in long dark coats and black wide-brimmed hats. Some had payot sidelocks – long curls of hair that grew down the sides of their faces as a sign that they were devout Jews. All had

beards. And Yossi was stunned by their appearance. It all came back to him. Holy days at home. Jewish people dressed so smartly. He'd forgotten this world even existed. In fact, he assumed that everyone who looked like this had been killed.

Yossi wasn't sure how to react as the men began to approach and speak to the boys nearest to them. For a second Yossi thought that he saw his father again. The man was thin with dark hair. Stooping. But before Yossi could call out, he saw it was not his father but another man. Why did this keep happening to him?

Now Mordecai was pulling at Yossi's shirt. "I need to speak to them," he demanded. "Come with me."

Yossi wasn't sure he wanted to. He shuddered. He looked around for Leo, but Leo was now talking to some other boys.

"Yossi," Mordecai pleaded.

Yossi knew that Mordecai rarely asked for anything. If he asked, he needed it rather than wanted it. Yossi also understood that Mordecai was far more religious than he was. He had told Yossi about his grandfather, how they would read the Bible together. He knew Mordecai prayed with the Rabbi and some other boys every morning before Yossi was even out of his bed.

So Yossi went with his friend.

They walked across the grass to approach one of the men. The man smiled and invited them to sit with him, explaining that he was from a city called Leeds just over a hundred miles away and that they were here to meet the boys and tell them about their community.

Mordecai leaned forward and fired question after question at the man, hardly giving him a

chance to speak. Yossi was glad of it – he had no desire to join in.

"You live in a Jewish town?" asked Mordecai.

"Many of us are Jewish," the man replied. "But there are lots of other people too. It is a large city with a Jewish community."

"A ghetto? Why have you been allowed out?"

The man smiled sadly and put his hand onto Mordecai's shoulder. "We are free. Here we are with you today. Leeds is not a ghetto. We live there by choice. In our own homes."

"Is there a school?" Mordecai went on.

"There are many schools."

"And Jews are allowed to go to school?"

"To the synagogue school or the national school. It's their choice. And in the evening, to the Cheder, the school where they study Judaism and the Bible."

Mordecai was silent for a few moments.

"Were many of you killed?" he asked the man at last.

The man shook his head. "None of us have been killed," he almost whispered. "Not here in England. Some went to fight. But they died away from here."

"Is there a synagogue then? You said a synagogue school."

"Yes, we have a synagogue. It is beautiful. And when you're inside, you feel so close to God. You know?"

Yossi saw his friend frown then nod.

"And tonight there will be a service here," the man went on. "We are inviting any of you boys who wish to join us, to come to worship tonight at sundown. To celebrate Rosh Hashanah. It is Friday. The Sabbath."

Yossi remembered these words. Rosh Hashanah. Sabbath. They were like distant echoes of something

before. He wanted to turn away. But he knew Mordecai felt differently.

Mordecai was staring at the floor.

"You have suffered terribly," the man said to him, his hand again on Mordecai's shoulder.

Mordecai seemed to be in a trance, tapping his feet, jerking his head.

"Can I ask you something more?" Mordecai said at last.

"Of course, my boy."

Mordecai eyed Yossi. And Yossi sensed that his friend was uneasy about him listening, that maybe he wanted to talk with the man privately.

Yossi jumped to his feet. "I need to go," he announced.

Then he jogged back across the grass, thrilled to get away. As he ran he noticed Joyce's mum at her window, gazing out towards the main road. Yossi felt

sad. He knew she was watching, waiting for her son to return.

Yossi sat at a distance as Mordecai spoke with the man. It was early evening, the sun had dropped behind the hills to the west and the day's light was slowly fading. He shivered and watched as a flock of hundreds of small black birds spiralled above the camp, then disappeared into the trees, tweeting and jabbering, invisible among the leaves.

Yossi thought about the idea of going to the religious service but immediately felt his body cramping, panicking. No, he wouldn't. He couldn't. Where were the swallows? he thought, trying to distract himself. They should be out now, catching flies above the lake and fields.

But there were none.

They had gone.

Before long Yossi saw that the men and the boys they had been speaking to were on the move, walking over to the main hall of the Calgarth Estate.

Mordecai walked up to him and put his hand out. Yossi took it and allowed his friend to pull him up from the grass.

"We're going in. For the service." Mordecai smiled. He looked happy, excited.

Yossi released Mordecai's hand.

"Come on," Mordecai said. "You said you'd come."

Yossi shook his head. "I can't," he said.

"What?" Mordecai looked confused. "Why?"

"I just can't," Yossi told him.

The two boys parted. Mordecai walking, almost running, to the room where the service would be held. Yossi going to sit under a tree and stare at the

ground. He would not go to the service. He could not go to the service. And he never would again.

*

In the ghetto, there had been a synagogue, centuries old. Torah scrolls inside an ornate wooden Ark. A menorah. All of them on a raised platform at the front of the congregation. Yossi had been to services there. Worshipped there on special occasions.

But – as with everything – the Nazis had destroyed it. Raided the synagogue, smashed it, piled up all the scrolls and books, doused them in petrol, then burned the papers and the synagogue to the ground.

They did it on a Friday at nightfall. Just so it hurt all the more.

But that destruction didn't stop the Jewish

leaders creating a new synagogue. The next one was in a cellar. A back room without windows. You were not supposed to speak about it, even to people in your family, in case you were overheard.

But someone must have spoken, someone must have been overheard.

Yossi was sitting outside the secret synagogue with his sisters, waiting for their grandfather – his father's father – who was praying, when a car arrived.

Four men in black uniforms jumped out of the car. They walked purposefully down the basement steps. Yossi's first instinct was to look after his two younger sisters. He made them stand up and retreated with them across the square to an alleyway. Now there were people between them and what was about to happen in the secret synagogue.

For a few seconds there was silence after the SS men had disappeared from view.

Then shouting.

Gunfire.

Wailing.

Now the SS men were coming up the steps again, forcing half a dozen older men and the Rabbi in front of them, making them carry the scrolls and the books. His grandfather was among them. Yossi's first impulse was to help, to stop this happening. But then he remembered the lady who had tried to help the man with the long beard who was beaten, remembered that his first duty was to keep his sisters safe.

Yossi's grandfather gave him a wild hopeless look across the square, then gestured that Yossi should leave. The SS men were kicking at their victims now, forcing them to stumble and fall in the street, then finally spill their precious cargo. The people who had filled the square disappeared, so

that the old men were left helpless and at the mercy
of the four SS soldiers.

Yossi had a clear view now: he could see his
grandfather sitting on the ground, looking down
at his shoes. Yossi was paralysed with fear, with
indecision. What should he do to stop this? What
could anyone do? He had to think of his sisters first,
not his grandfather.

"Go down the alleyway," he told Anna and Mina.
There was a small shop where those who still had
money were able to buy vegetables. "To the shop. I
will follow."

Now Yossi watched from the corner of a
building. One of the SS men bent down to start a
fire. Soon flames were consuming the books and
scrolls as their seven helpless victims sat or stood
limp, heads down.

The fire burning well now, the soldiers turned

to face the Rabbi and the other old men. Yossi could hear their shouts and laughter, but he couldn't bear to watch what would happen next. How could God let this happen?

*

"Are you feeling well?" One of the Jewish men from Leeds interrupted Yossi's thoughts.

"Yes," Yossi said, lying.

"Do you want to speak of something? You look troubled."

Yossi shook his head.

"Will you come and worship with us?" the man asked.

"I cannot," Yossi said.

TWELVE

Then came the day that Yossi had been waiting for. The Red Cross arrived at the estate to speak to them.

"During the war ... most of you were separated from your parents and other members of your families. You may have some ideas about what happened to your loved ones. You may not. But I thank all of you for supplying the names and details that you have. It is *our* job at the Red Cross to try to find any surviving members of your families."

Yossi leaned forward, Leo on his left, Mordecai on his right, in a hall of three hundred children, all desperate to hear news.

"The most likely time you would have lost them is when – and if – you were kept in a ghetto in your town or a neighbouring town. In the clearing of the ghettos, as you well know, many families were separated."

Yossi remembered.

"Or," the lady from the Red Cross went on, "at the next stage, when you were transported to the concentration camps. You may have lost touch with family then."

She paused.

"I am sorry to remind you of these events. But if you can remember where and when you last saw your loved ones, then it might help us re-connect you."

Yossi understood. He had been waiting for the opportunity to find his father and be reunited.

The Red Cross lady went on: "Now that the war

is over across Europe, many people are returning from the East. Thousands of people from your home countries fled to Russia, where many of them were lucky enough to escape and survive. It is possible that some of your family are among those returning.

"Some were taken in by kind people, who kept them hidden throughout the war. Others escaped into the forests. Others still fought as partisans, hiding in the forests and attacking the Germans ... so, the chances of *someone* being alive out there are not impossible but ... and this is hard to say ... please do not build up too much hope. We are finding that it is a struggle to reunite people because, in many cases, their loved ones are no longer there."

The lady bowed her head, took a sip of water, then looked up again. Yossi studied her face as he listened to her voice. She was calm and clear.

"But we will not stop trying until we have exhausted every possibility," she went on. "There is ... some ... hope. And we must all hold on to the hope that one day some of you will see your fathers, mothers, sisters and brothers again."

Yossi had hope. His mind was chaos. Everything the woman had said had brought on another surge of memories. The ghetto. The liquidation of the ghetto. The train.

*

It had all happened suddenly. Very early in the morning in the ghetto. There was noise from the street. Yossi heard shouting, then shooting. He leapt from the mattress he shared with his two sisters to find his father peering down from the window at men banging on doors.

Everyone was to report to the square. To bring only what they could carry. They were leaving.

Hundreds of them were marched out of the ghetto and made to board trains. They were told they were going to a new place, a better place. There would be suitable accommodation there. There would be proper food.

All of it lies. But at the time they hoped it would be true. They didn't imagine things could get worse than in the ghetto.

Onto the trains. Forced at gunpoint or by the blow of a rifle butt.

Yossi shuddered. It was no ordinary railway journey. He was with Mina and Anna and his mother and father in a wooden truck meant for carrying cattle to the slaughterhouse. Two days on a train with no windows, the closed wooden carriages packed so full of people that nobody could sit down.

Two days without food or water. No toilets. Barely able to breathe in the summer heat. All the time his father reassuring them it would be worth it to get to the new place.

Those two awful nights on the train were to be the last two nights Yossi spent with his mother and sisters. He still remembered how good it felt at one point to be holding Mina in his arms so she could sleep. He would never forget. The man next to him had collapsed, but there was no room for him to fall, so he had been leaning against Yossi all night. It was only in the morning, when they were released from the truck, that he realised the man was dead. It was not something Yossi had shared with Mina.

When their horrific journey was finally over, Yossi and his family emerged from the cramped stinking cattle trucks feeling relief as well as fear.

They had been told they were being

transported to a new ghetto. But this place didn't look like a ghetto. They were in the middle of the countryside, far away from any city.

The name of the place, they learned, was Auschwitz.

As soon as they got off the train, they were forced forwards by German soldiers with long wooden sticks. Anyone who argued was beaten, sometimes until their body was dragged away and Yossi wasn't able to tell if they were merely unconscious or dead.

Amid the chaos of shouting and crying and the threats from the German soldiers, a thin man sidled up to Yossi and whispered, "Tell them you have a trade. Tell them you're a tailor. Just say something. Save yourself." Yossi had no idea what the man meant, but he could see people ahead of him being questioned by the soldiers.

There was mud on the ground, so deep that the moisture seeped into Yossi's old shoes. There was a smell like an overflowing toilet as he found himself funnelled to the front of the mass of people who had been forced from the train. They were now being separated into two queues by the soldiers. All around him was the noise of people crying and shouting "No".

"Age?" Yossi was asked by one of the soldiers. He was eleven.

"Fourteen," Yossi replied, standing on his tiptoes and puffing his chest out, while watching a man in the right-hand queue collapse, then be dragged away, beaten and forced to stand in the left-hand queue.

He did what his mother had told him to do. Lie about his age. Make himself look bigger.

"Trade?"

"Tailor," Yossi gasped, panicking but grateful to have an answer to give.

Having been sent to the right-hand queue, Yossi looked round to make sure that his parents and sisters were still behind him.

His father was. His mother too. They were ordered into the right-hand queue behind Yossi. But Mina and Anna were ordered to the left, both of them standing with their arms dangling at their sides, pale-faced, staring at their mother. The noise of their crying was drowned out by the sound of other people crying, shouting, calling out.

Next, he saw his mother and father's hands touching, then separating as his mother moved left to be with his sisters.

"No," Yossi heard himself shout.

Yossi feared that he knew what the queue on the right meant. There was a phrase he had heard one of the soldiers say: *fit for work*. Yossi knew he was in the fit for work queue. But he didn't know what

happened to the people in the other queue on the left. The women. The girls. The old people. What could you do if you weren't fit for work? Where did you go?

And he also didn't know why his mother had gone to join his sisters. She was still a youngish woman. *She* could work. He went to go and tell her, grabbing her, pulling her away from Mina and Anna across the divide.

"Leave me," his mother said calmly to him. Then she whispered something in his ear that chilled him to the bone but made him move away, looking at each of them solemnly in the eyes: Mina, Anna, his mother.

"Your mother will look after your sisters," his father said.

"I understand."

"She must," Yossi's father croaked. "They need a parent. You have me and they have your mother."

"I know, Dad," Yossi said.

Yossi's father put his hands on his shoulders, as if he was comforting him. But Yossi knew better. He could feel the full weight of his father's frame leaning on him now. Without Yossi there, his father would have collapsed in front of everyone, could maybe have been taken to the left-hand side too, deemed *not* fit for work.

Yossi stood still, looking again at his mother. The words she had whispered to him echoed in his head like she had shouted them across a valley.

"You must leave me," she had said. "And you must live, Yossi. You must survive. Only you can keep the family line going now."

She had given him a hint that he might survive. But in doing so she had foretold what would happen to Mina, to Anna and to herself.

THIRTEEN

Towards the end of September there was a storm over Windermere. A violent one. The noise of the thunder rolling off the mountains surrounding the lake was almost exactly the same as the explosion of the bombs Yossi had heard in the camps.

The heavens opened and rain fell so hard that Yossi wondered if it was possible for the lake water to rise up the hillsides, submerging everyone and everything in this valley and the next. He wondered what the birds and animals would do if there was no land. He thought about Noah and his ark. Then he stopped worrying and joined the dozens of children

as they ran wildly along the banks of Trout Beck, down to the lake where most of the older children had gathered to marvel at waist-high waves crashing onto the shore.

There was electricity in the air. Excitement. It was like the lightning above had charged the children, who were running round and round in the watery fields, whooping and laughing. Dorothy's little girl, Joyce, and some of her school friends were there with Spot, and the small white dog was sprinting in circles in and out of the shallow water, yapping.

Yossi tried to catch Spot until he had to give up and put his hands on his knees to catch his breath. He was gasping for air. Just a short run and he was shattered.

"Keep back," Jock Lawrence called.

The sports teacher had been overseeing a swimming session with a group of boys he called his

Swimming Team. "The lake's angry today. It could snatch you and drag you in if you're not careful."

When they returned to the Calgarth Estate, soaked to the skin, Yossi, Mordecai and Leo saw the younger children standing at the door to their building. Their faces were fearful, like they had been when Yossi had seen them on the first morning at breakfast. It was rare to see the younger ones out at all. Normally, they stayed indoors, too scared to go outside.

The thunder and rain had stopped now. The younger children – a mixture of girls and boys – wanted to experience the watery world and take part in the frenzy the adults had kept them away from. Trout Beck had burst its banks, waterlogging the fields up to the buildings. The children came out to splash in the grass with Marie. Talia was there, beckoning Yossi.

"Help with the young ones?" she pleaded.

Yossi, Leo and Mordecai did as they were asked. Yossi walked shyly alongside the children as they waded ankle-deep in water. Mordecai, pointing at plants and leaves, tried to teach them English words.

But it was Leo the children wanted to be with. He started by walking along beside them on his knees, making himself the same height. They laughed and screamed and walked behind him in a comical line, grinning. Before long he was lying down in the water, pretending he was having a bath, making out that he was washing his armpits and then his face with the flood water.

The children howled with laughter as Leo took them closer to the stream. Marie and Talia watched on, smiling.

Once the children were tired, Yossi and the others helped Marie and Talia to dry them off. They

had large white towels and wrapped the children up in them. Leo put a towel over his head and ran around chasing the children. Mordecai and Yossi did the same, following their friend's lead, to more laughter and more looks of approval from Talia and Marie.

Next they started a pillow fight, leaving six of the younger children on the bed, bashing each other, falling over, laughing, jumping up again. Then the three boys joined Talia and Marie for a cup of tea.

"You are three very good boys," Marie told them. "I can't thank you enough. We've made such progress with the young ones today. Who'd have thought that a thunderstorm could encourage the children outside rather than the sunshine?"

With the children's laughter as background noise, they talked for a while about how the lake had been so wild.

Yossi gazed out of the window. There were a

few seconds of silence until he noticed Marie looking at Talia with a puzzled expression on her face.

"What is it?" she asked.

"They're quiet," Marie said. "The children."

"Exhausted?" Talia suggested. "Asleep?"

Marie didn't look so sure.

Yossi stood up. He was nearest to the room where they'd been having their pillow fight.

"I'll check," he said, and went to see if the children were all right. He peeped into the room to see a huddle in the middle of the bed, a cloud of tiny feathers falling softly from a burst pillow. The children were gazing in silent awe at the feathers, smiling and wafting them as they fell onto the bed.

Yossi had to try hard not to collapse at the sight. He didn't want the children to see his reaction to what they thought was something lovely.

The memory that came this time was brutal.

*

That first day in the concentration camp. After being split up from his mother and sisters, Yossi and his father had been forced into a long wooden hut. They were with dozens of men and boys. Some were talking in low voices, others lying waiting. One man was laughing and talking to himself.

They sat with other men on the floor and his father hit his head softly against the wall, eyes closed, barely able to look at his son.

Then millions of grey flakes began to fall from the sky. Ash. Yossi saw them through the doorway. The door was quickly closed to keep the flakes out of the building.

"What are they, Dad?" Yossi had asked.

His dad shook his head, eyes screwed shut.

The laughing man had wild dark-rimmed eyes.

Seeing Yossi, he came to crouch next to him. He was still giggling.

"That's your mother and your sisters," he told Yossi.

*

Yossi shook the memory from his mind. He had to think of these children first, keep them from seeing his distress.

"Go out now," he said gently, swallowing back the impulse to vomit. "Go to Marie."

The children did as he urged, leaving Yossi alone with the falling feathers. He sat on the bed, then began softly knocking his head against the wall until his friends – Mordecai and Leo – came to stand beside him.

FOURTEEN

"Are you coming?"

It was Mordecai. He had knocked at Yossi's bedroom door the morning after the episode with the burst pillow and was standing there now, expecting his friend to join him for breakfast as he had every day since they arrived at Windermere. This morning he was wearing his yarmulke, a small cap on his head, indicating to Yossi that his friend had been to pray with the Rabbi and some other boys, although Mordecai seemed to wear it all the time now, showing his increasing religious devotion.

"Not today," Yossi said, turning away to face the

wall. "I'm not going to get up. Today I am going to lie in bed all day."

"Oh ... that's ... well, that's fine. I'll see you later," Mordecai said. After hesitating, he closed the door softly.

Yossi heard Leo and Mordecai's voices fade into the babble of the conversations of dozens of children heading for breakfast as he lay there, his teeth clenched.

He knew that Mordecai would speak to Talia and that she would come to see if he was all right. But he still lay there, determined not to get up. Why should he? After what he had seen the afternoon before.

Ten minutes later, another knock at the door.

"Yossi. It's Talia. Can I come in?"

"No."

"Yossi?"

After a minute, Yossi's door opened, the hinge squealing like it always did.

"Are you coming for breakfast?" Talia asked.

"No."

"You have to, Yossi," Talia said. "You need to eat."

"I don't need to eat. I ate three times yesterday. Four times."

"And you must eat again."

"Not today. I'm not getting up or eating or doing anything today."

"And why's that?"

"Why?" Yossi sat up and looked at Talia, full of rage. "Why should I? After everything I've been through. After the last six years ... why should I get up and eat breakfast? Why should I wash my face and brush my teeth? Why not just lie here instead? Everyone is dead. My mother, my sisters, my uncles,

aunts, grandmothers, grandfathers, cousins, half
cousins. I don't know if my father is dead or alive.
What is going to happen to me in a month, in six
months? We have to leave here soon and I don't
know what will happen when we do. But I do know
I can just lie here and it feels all right. I am weak. I
can hardly run or swim without losing my breath.
Why get up and feel so tired that I just want to come
back to bed?"

It all came out in one great splurge of anger.

Talia listened without replying, although she did
step back.

Fearing that he had scared her, Yossi despaired
and curled his body up into a ball under his bedding.
He had surprised himself.

"You mustn't give up," Talia pleaded. "The Red
Cross are coming again soon. They will be looking
for the names you gave them. There could still be

people who have given them *your* name. There might be someone from your family. Someone out there."

"I'm not giving up," Yossi snapped. "I'm just not *getting* up."

"I'll come back later," Talia said calmly. "Maybe you should go to see the doctor?"

"There's no point," Yossi told her.

As Yossi saw the door close, he heard laughter and shouts from outside, the noise of a vehicle coming into the estate and a bird's song that he didn't recognise. Normally he would have wanted to know who was arriving in the vehicle or to try to identify the bird. But not today. Today, he lay there, stubbornly disengaged from the world. Didn't he have a right to be angry? Who on this planet had a better excuse to just lie in bed than him?

Then, in his head, he heard a voice.

"I know it's cold, Yossi. It's freezing. But we have

to get up and wash. We have to look after ourselves. If we don't wash, if we let ourselves go, the Germans will think that they were right: that we are not human."

Yossi opened his eyes.

It had been before sunrise in the deep of winter. Dark. Freezing cold. Hunger gnawing at his stomach. He had been lying there shivering, wanting an extra five minutes without moving, holding on to half-sleep. He hadn't wanted to wash his face. Until his father said that.

Yossi closed his eyes. How could he have forgotten? To get up and wash his face was the only thing he could do to fight back against the Nazis. They had taken his village, his home, his bicycle, his school. They had taken his mother and his sisters. Washing his face and getting up, defiant, was his act of resistance. It had been then and it must be now.

FIFTEEN

Yossi stood and waited his turn outside the doctor's surgery. There were six wooden chairs in a row, with a low table in front of them and a copy of the local newspaper for patients to read.

Yossi had made a decision while washing and brushing his teeth.

After his initial health check the night they arrived from Prague on the Stirling bomber, he had not seen the doctor. He had not been ill, so there had been no need. But now he wanted some advice.

The doctor's name was Patterdale. He was a small man. Small and thin.

"How can I help you ...?" The doctor glanced at a brown file that he had on his desk. "Yossi."

"I want to be strong," Yossi told the doctor, wondering what was in the file.

Doctor Patterdale nodded and studied Yossi in silence. Yossi took the chance to look around the surgery. He saw a picture of the human body with blue and red veins drawn onto it. And a full-size model of a skeleton dangling from a metal hook. Yossi looked away from the skeleton. It was too real. Too much like the corpses on the streets of the ghetto that he had become used to walking past.

The doctor had not yet replied, so Yossi felt compelled to say more.

"I would like to be strong and fit," Yossi said again. "Like Jock Lawrence. Like the pilot who brought me over here. I could be a pilot, maybe? But not if I am weak, like this."

"Let's have a look at you, shall we?" the doctor said.

Over the next few minutes Doctor Patterdale took Yossi's pulse, weighed him, studied his skin, shone a light into his eyes and ears, felt his stomach and the organs beneath Yossi's ribcage, his legs and arms. To Yossi it felt like the doctor was searching for something beneath the surface, something hidden that would reveal a truth about Yossi, something that he could take out to make Yossi well.

"You've had a lot of physical activity, but repetitive work," Doctor Patterdale told him. "Walking. Using your arms. Did you work in a factory in the camps?"

Yossi nodded. He understood most of what the doctor was saying. He had a sharp short memory of working in the factory that was part of the concentration camp where he was kept first with his

father. Pushing the same heavy trolley every day, the aching in his joints and bones at night.

Pointing at parts of his body to help Yossi understand, the doctor went on: "Your skin, your eyes, your gums and teeth show signs of malnutrition. Hunger, yes? Not enough to eat? But you're a good weight now. You are recovering."

Yossi looked at himself in the mirror. His face was round. His stomach too. His arms were chubby.

"You have had food," Patterdale looked at his notes again, "at Theresienstadt. Rice pudding, I believe?"

"Yes," Yossi said.

"From the Russians?"

"Yes. Every meal. Rice pudding. Every day."

"So you have a lot of body fat but very little muscle." The doctor squeezed the fat on Yossi's arm. "Your joints are poor." He tapped Yossi's knee, then

his ankle. "This is why you are unfit. What you need is daily exercise. Swimming. Walking. Slow running. Yes?"

The doctor acted out each sport so Yossi would understand.

"Thank you, Doctor."

"And eat meat, fish, chicken and eggs when you can get your hands on them. Don't fill up on white bread. Eat vegetables for minerals and vitamins. But I think they feed you well here. So, first and foremost, exercise. Go and see Jock Lawrence. He'll help you."

The doctor looked at the door and Yossi realised his appointment was over. He stood up.

"Thank you," he said. He had understood most of what the doctor said. Enough to show him the way.

"My pleasure, Yossi," Doctor Patterdale said. "Please come back and see me any time."

Outside the building, Yossi watched clouds move rapidly across the tops of the hills on the other side of the lake. The scene reminded him of the Carpathian Mountains in Poland, where, while on holiday in the summers, he and his father and sisters used to walk all day. When he was fit and strong. Before the war.

Yossi gritted his teeth. This was it. He would become fit and strong again. And he would begin today.

After lunch, Yossi joined Jock Lawrence's swimming group.

"All set, boys?" Lawrence asked.

Twenty-two boys grinned and picked up their bags and towels. Talia had also come along, as usual, to translate what Lawrence had to say.

Then they walked along the track that led to

the lake shore. Although it was sunny, there was a wind coming from the top of the lake, ruffling the trees. A cool wind.

"The doctor spoke to me," Lawrence said to Yossi as they walked together at the back of the boisterous group of boys.

Yossi looked at their sports coach. His arms were like ropes. Hard and muscular. He noticed Lawrence was looking him up and down too.

"It will take time," Lawrence cautioned. "You can't go from what you've been through and then start swimming across the lake in one day."

"How long?" Yossi asked.

Lawrence smiled. "The important thing is not to start too fast. Today and the next few times, just doing it is enough. Build some strength with the exercises we're going to do. Swim a little. Just get used to the movement. Dr Patterdale said your joints

are weak. So work on moving first, build them up before you force your muscles."

They arrived at the water. The light changed as they emerged from the trees, sunshine skimming off the surface of the lake. Yossi shielded his eyes. This scenery. It never stopped amazing him.

"I understand," Yossi said.

"And you want to become a pilot?" Lawrence asked. "The doctor said."

"Maybe," Yossi replied.

"My brother was in the RAF," Lawrence told him.

"A pilot?" Yossi asked enthusiastically.

"No," Lawrence said. "A tail-end Charlie."

"I don't understand."

"A gunner, yes? In the rear of the plane." Lawrence put both his arms out in front of him and shook them as if he was shooting a large gun.

"Yes. I understand," Yossi said.

Lawrence stared across the lake and frowned.

Yossi had another question.

"Has your brother ever said how aeroplanes can take off?"

Jock Lawrence smiled. "He did. He said that the aeroplane keeps going on the airfield, building up more and more power before it can lift off. It takes time, but once it has enough power, it leaves the ground."

Yossi thought he understood. He knew that some of what Lawrence had been trying to tell him was lost in translation, but he understood all the same.

"He said that?"

"He did," Lawrence nodded, still gazing at the water.

And something occurred to Yossi: how sad Lawrence looked when he spoke about his brother.

"Is your brother dead?" Yossi asked.

"He is."

"I'm sorry."

Lawrence smiled. "Thank you. He was flying over Germany in a Lancaster. They must have been hit by anti-aircraft fire. But he wanted to do it. I think he was a little like you, maybe?"

Yossi remembered seeing Lancaster bombers over one of the concentration camps he'd been in. He knew what they looked like because one of the men in the camp had been in the German army before he was discovered to be a Jew, and he could identify the planes. He'd told Yossi that now the bombers were able to come over German territory as far as the camps, it meant that the Nazis were losing the war in the air, maybe losing the war overall.

So seeing those planes meant everything to Yossi. They were a sign, high in the sky, that the

Germans were being defeated, that this nightmare might nearly be over, that soon – very soon – they might be free. That was why Yossi loved aeroplanes.

Yossi wondered if Lawrence would want to know. He took a risk.

"I saw them," Yossi said in English. "The Lancaster bombers. They came to save us. Your brother. Maybe I saw his aeroplane?"

"Maybe," Lawrence smiled.

"Your brother," Yossi said, "he is a hero. Thank you."

SIXTEEN

It was the middle of October. All lessons took place indoors now, and even inside the buildings cold air would play around their ankles. Instead of lounging around in shorts and shirts, most of the boys now wore jackets and long trousers inside and out.

They were learning about England. What sort of jobs you could do. How you could get an education. Who could help them as they tried to start their new lives.

Outside, the weather had taken a turn for the worse over the last week. Great sheets of rain would come pouring out of the skies most days, like waterfalls coming off the mountains.

And then there was the light. Or lack of it, the sun sometimes barely making it over the top of the hills. Inside the classrooms and halls it was darker. Even in their bedrooms. The mood among the children on the Calgarth Estate dipped. The lake was ice cold; few of the boys fancied swimming.

There was a lot of talk now among the children about what was going to happen to them next. Yossi had heard some of the boys talking about Palestine, a part of the world where Jews could live and finally be safe. Others favoured staying in England and becoming part of a Jewish community in one of the larger cities like Leeds, Manchester or Gateshead. Yossi knew that Mordecai was thinking about moving to Leeds to join the community he'd heard about from the men who had come to see them.

In addition, there was still no news from the Red Cross. Yossi wondered if they had been able to

trace any of those names that the children had so diligently listed in their exercise books.

Maybe some letter or card was in a van now weaving its way to them. Like Dorothy, Yossi often looked out at the road to see what was coming. He wasn't the only one of the children to do so.

But he knew, deep down, it was too soon. How many names were there to check? How many different places across the world were there surviving Jews?

After the lesson, Yossi followed Leo and Mordecai out of the classroom and onto the grass outside, where they could hear voices and the thud of a football being kicked – a game was underway now that the rain had stopped.

Yossi studied the football match and the players and quickly realised that this was no casual game of football being played between meals and lessons.

This was different.

Over the weeks, the children had broken into distinct groups. Friends with friends. Poles with Poles. Czechs with Czechs. They ate together, were educated together and played games together. Usually football.

One very distinct group was the German boys who stuck closely together. Yossi understood why. Polish boys stuck together. Czech boys did. Friendship groups were formed around language first. That was normal. Yossi also knew that the Germans were Jewish, like all the others, and that they had suffered just as much as he and his friends had done during the war. There were German Jews and there were Polish Jews. It hadn't made any difference to the Nazis in the camps: they wanted all Jews dead.

The Germans were playing against some of the

older Polish boys. To Yossi, neither team looked like it was made up of boys; they were more like men. Ever since they had come to Windermere they had all been growing. They ate well. They had exercise. They were no longer slaves.

Yossi could feel his arms and legs and chest were bigger and stronger when he showered now. He sometimes looked at himself in the mirror and noticed his neck was thicker. It felt strange.

Yossi joined Leo on the touchline, watching as the game became more intense.

It didn't take long for the trouble to start.

A wiry Polish winger found space wide and looked to have broken past the last defender, Heinrich. The German defender looked furious at the way he'd been fooled and he lunged, two-footed, at the winger speeding past him.

Contact.

The Polish player screamed out in pain, then
rolled over two or three times before stopping
in a heap. Immediately two of the Polish boy's
team-mates were in Heinrich's face.

"You pig," the one with blond hair said. "You
could have broken his leg."

Heinrich was laughing.

One of the Poles swung at him and caught
his face, but Heinrich was too big to go down. Now
he stood large over his two assailants, one of his
team-mates at his shoulder.

"Back off. It was an accident," Heinrich told
them.

But the blond Polish boy was still going at him,
encouraged by his team-mates who were pushing
and shoving some of the other Germans.

Now more players became involved.

"That wasn't an accident!" The fouled player

could be heard now, his voice high-pitched and indignant. "You did it on purpose. You couldn't help yourself, you Nazi scum."

This boy had now got back up and pushed Heinrich so hard that he was lying curled up. He had his arms up to protect his head, but his adversary was astride him, leaning in and punching left, right, left, right, one fist after another.

It was brutal.

Yossi could hear a crunch with the impact of each fist.

Blood.

Broken teeth.

Everyone had abandoned the game and was standing in a circle. Watching. No one intervened. And then the screams of pain stopped.

Heinrich was no longer fighting back, though his Polish assailant continued to loom over him.

But still no one came forward to help him.

Except Leo, who now ran at the Polish boy and – putting all his strength and weight and will into it – kicked him so hard he somersaulted off Heinrich. Then Leo was standing over the Polish player, shouting over and over.

"*Stirb, du Schwein! Stirb, du Schwein!*"

For Yossi, it was like time had frozen. Everyone on the estate had stopped. People weren't walking. Vehicles weren't driving. There was no noise. It was as if Leo had broken some fixed rule of the universe and the world had stopped turning. Only Jock Lawrence was moving, sprinting from the main building over to where the fight had broken out.

And within these few seconds of silence, Yossi's mind was running like a film reel with a scene from one of the factories inside Auschwitz, where Yossi had first met Leo and Mordecai.

*

The factory made brushes. For polishing German soldiers' boots. For brushing down German horses and whatever else the German army needed brushes for. In Yossi's mind he could see the four of them standing there: himself, Mordecai, Leo and Aaron, Leo's older brother.

A guard was shouting in their faces because on the floor in front of them was a jumble of hundreds of pieces of wood and binding and bristles that had been knocked noisily from a rack. This was a catastrophe for whoever was responsible – or for all of them. Anyone who made a mistake like this could expect a beating. Or worse.

Leo had done it. The four boys all knew that. He had fallen asleep on his feet or fainted from hunger and crashed into the boxes containing the brushes and

bristles. They fell and scattered, making such a racket that the Nazi guards were onto them immediately.

"Which of you has done this?" one guard was screaming.

None of them answered.

"Which of you? You will all die if you don't tell me now."

Still they stood with their heads down. All of them.

Yossi remembered what happened next. He would never forget. One of them stepped forward.

Aaron.

"I did it," he said.

Without there being time for Leo to contradict his brother, Aaron was grabbed by the hair, thrown to the floor, kicked in his stomach, back, groin and face, and beaten hard with the butt of the soldier's rifle.

"Stirb, du Schwein! Stirb, du Schwein!" were

the words the guard used as he kicked and stamped on Leo's brother. It seemed to go on for ever. Unrelenting. All the while Yossi, Mordecai and Leo stood staring at their feet until Aaron was dead and his body was dragged away, like one of the sacks they used to clear up the rubbish, and the three of them understood they had to return to their work or suffer the same.

*

That night after the football match a group of the boys met by the lake.

No adults were invited.

Footballers from several different countries were there. Yossi recognised Poles, Czechs, Germans, Hungarians and others. He and Mordecai stood at a slight distance, watching. But Leo was involved.

The sky was clear. The moonlight was enough

to see by as it reflected off the lake in a million ripples. Yossi heard an owl hooting, marking out its territory.

The boys looped a rope over a low bough that was about ten foot above them, dry autumn leaves falling off the branch. Leo made sure it was secure, then he handed it to Heinrich, the German boy he had rescued that afternoon.

Now – together – several boys came forward to play their part in the ceremony. They were carrying a figure dressed in a black jacket and long trousers. Yossi couldn't imagine where they'd got the long trousers from. The figure's head was misshapen but still looked human.

They attached the figure to the rope by the neck, then Leo pulled the rope to haul it up. Against the moonlit water the figure swung slightly until it was still. And none of the children said a word.

Yossi studied the figure dangling on the rope. Someone had drawn a small moustache on its face. There was no doubt who this suit stuffed with cloth and paper was meant to be.

Adolf Hitler.

After a few moments, Heinrich took a box of matches out of his pocket and lit one of the screwed-up paper legs sticking out of the bottom of the trousers.

The effigy caught fire very quickly.

Yossi watched, fascinated, as flames rippled up the legs and the chest. And now, in the darkness, he could see the faces of the dozens of boys, their eyes reflecting the flames, blackness all around them as the moon hid behind a cloud.

SEVENTEEN

The next morning Yossi, Mordecai and Leo went for a walk up Sallows Fell, a hill that overlooked Windermere. It was Leo's idea, but Yossi was pleased to go along with it. Hiking was one of the things Doctor Patterdale had suggested he do.

They walked up the hill behind the Calgarth Estate. It was a low fell, not one of the snow-dusted mountains to the west. But it still felt steep and hard on Yossi's legs. The mud was frozen and cracked under their feet before giving way.

"I have a thought," Leo told them, breaking the

silence once they were away from Calgarth. "I want to live in Palestine."

Yossi stopped in his tracks. He felt a sudden urge to lash out, push his friend down the hillside. Where had he got this idea? Leo now wanted to live in Palestine? He had plans that didn't involve Yossi or Mordecai?

"No, you can't do that," Yossi snapped. He felt sick with anxiety that he might lose Leo.

But Leo carried on explaining: "I ... I want you two to come with me to Palestine. I want *you* to be safe. And I happen to think that you will be safest in Palestine. With me."

Yossi softened the tone of his voice. "I see."

"Yeah," Leo coughed.

"So why Palestine?" Yossi asked.

Leo threw up his arms. "Because it is the only country in the world that we know where they don't go

after Jews, maybe? A place we can live safely and not feel like we are unwelcome guests. A land of our own."

"And here?" Yossi started to say. "We're safe here, aren't we?"

"There are people here in England who don't like Jews, too," Leo interrupted. "Heinrich told me. There's a fascist party here. In the cities. They're everywhere. And we have to leave Windermere soon. In a month, maybe. We might have to go to a city. Let's see how they treat Jews there. And we can't go home, Yossi. You know I went back. In Poland. Even with the Germans gone, they still want to kill us."

Yossi shook his head. "But the war is over," he said.

"You didn't go back," Leo snapped. "Did you? Back to Poland? Like I did."

Neither Yossi nor Mordecai answered. They weren't sure they wanted to hear what Leo had

to say about the time he had gone back to Poland immediately after the war. He'd never wanted to speak about it before. They walked on in silence, until Mordecai coughed and said, "I was thinking ... we could all go to Leeds. We should go there. The Jewish community there have offered us lodgings and the chance to learn a profession. They said they would look after us. Make us welcome."

"It's different in the cities," Leo said again. "It might not be safe ..."

Yossi stopped listening as Leo and Mordecai argued. What Leo had said about them having to move on soon, leave Windermere – it was true. And what would he do if he didn't hear from his father before then? They were still waiting for news from the Red Cross, but they couldn't stay here for ever. They would have to move on. To Leeds. To Palestine. Somewhere.

Where should he go? Who should he go with? His head hurt as he tried to think about the future, and his legs were aching now. This was the longest walk Yossi had done since leaving Auschwitz. That walk when he collapsed and his father disappeared. The pain in his legs now reminded him of it – and the heavy silence as they trudged back towards the estate. But Yossi knew from experience that he could walk like this for days if he had to. He might be tired, but this was not real tiredness, and no one was going to kill him if he stopped to rest or fell down exhausted.

*

One evening in the middle of January 1945, the guards ordered everybody onto the concentration camp square to be counted. They were told to bring all the clothes they could wear, but not what was happening. Then they were funnelled out of the gates

of Auschwitz, passing under the words written in wrought iron on the gate – *Arbeit Macht Frei* – and marched away.

Away from the Russian front line, which was moving ever closer. The prisoners in Auschwitz had begun to hear booms and bullet fire from the hills to the east. The rumours were it was the Russians advancing across Poland to liberate them. If they could just hold on, survive just a little longer, they would be free. The Nazis would be gone. It was only a matter of time. But now they were being marched away from their liberation. And to where? To what?

At times Yossi marched alongside his father. At others, between his friends, Leo and Mordecai. You had to stay alert. If you fell behind ... if you gave up ... if you fell over ... they shot you.

Yossi heard a gunshot every few minutes. It was normal. He knew what it meant. So you kept

marching. You endured the pain in your legs, the crippling cold and the hunger. You had no choice.

Having marched for a while with the help of his two friends, one foot in front of the other, Yossi wanted to find his father again, to make sure he was still away from the back of the marchers.

But he was not there.

He was nowhere.

No one could remember if he had moved forward looking for his son or if he had fallen back, stumbled. But somehow Yossi had carried on. He and Leo and Mordecai had managed to keep each other going.

*

The boys were still silent as they walked back to the Calgarth Estate. Passing the art block, Spot came bursting out of the door, pursued by shrieks and screams.

He looked different. Very different.

"He's— " Leo said, but was unable to get the words out before his clothes were smeared in colour as the dog jumped into his arms.

Spot was covered in paint. Red, blue, yellow, green. And he was rubbing it all over Leo.

Yossi looked over to see the younger children watching from the door, their faces creased with laughter. But Yossi didn't feel like laughing. All three of them were sullen, glum. Their conversation up the fell had left them with more questions than answers about their future.

"We should take him home, maybe?" Yossi said, after the dog had calmed down and the children had lost interest in the spectacle.

"We might get something to eat if we do," Leo nodded. "As a reward for bringing him home safely."

The three boys agreed to head over to Spot's

house without another word, remembering the warm welcome they'd been given the last time they had visited.

There, as usual, at the window of the small one-storey house was Dorothy, Joyce's mum. Cloth in hand, staring up to the main road. When she saw her dog, practical as ever she took Spot by the neck and doused him down in the small garden with a bucket of water.

"Thank you, boys," she said.

As Dorothy rubbed the rest of the paint off the dog with an old towel, Yossi gazed around her home, at the fire spluttering in the small hearth, at the photographs of Joyce and the one of her son, Peter, the soldier.

Feeling an ache deep inside his stomach, Yossi remembered his own home. They had a fireplace. They had photographs and cakes, a mum, a dad, a

family. He was keen to hear if Dorothy had had word from her son in the Far East.

"Have you heard from Peter?" Yossi asked. "Now the war has been over a long time?"

Joyce's mum looked uncomfortable for a moment. "Not yet," she smiled.

Yossi stared at Spot and thought about what it meant not to have heard from someone for a few months in a war.

"Do not the army tell you?" he asked her.

Dorothy shrugged. "No."

None of the boys knew what to say. It was one of those moments when everyone is paralysed but feels the pressure to say something.

Dorothy broke the silence.

"Did you ever try to go home?" she asked. "Once the war was over? Before you came here?"

Yossi shook his head quickly. Mordecai too.

They both expected Leo to do the same. But Leo was leaning forward, looking into Dorothy's eyes.

"After we were liberated, I go back to Poland," he told her.

Dorothy nodded and Yossi and Mordecai stared at their friend. Was he going to tell Dorothy what he'd not yet told them?

"I go south. Americans take me in jeep. Then Scottish soldiers took me to Krakow. Then I find a bus. The Scottish men give me money. All very kind. I reach my village. I walk down the street. It is nearly dark. And the synagogue is burned black and falling down. There is a family in my father's house. None of our neighbours are there any more. I know no one. After this I sit – tired, confused – and watch my home, and two men come from house. They say I have to go. They see my clothes. My hair is shaved short then. They know what I am. They

shout I do not live here any more. This is not my village any more. Then they chase me and hit me. They kick me on the floor. They say if I am there in morning, I die. I walk away. It's finished. Come back to Theresienstadt."

Silence again.

Yossi struggled to swallow the piece of scone in his mouth. Leo, trying to look relaxed, grabbed Spot and began to play fight with him.

Dorothy had walked away from them into the kitchen. She took the cloth from her shoulder and buried her face in it.

Yossi decided, at that moment, that he would go wherever Leo went, wherever Mordecai went. He didn't care if it was Leeds, Palestine or the moon.

EIGHTEEN

A few mornings later Mordecai burst into Yossi's room without knocking.

"They're here," he gasped.

For a few seconds Yossi was confused. Then he understood. Today was the day: the Red Cross day.

Yossi jumped out of bed and began to put his clothes on as quickly as he could, then scrambled to the washrooms. He wanted to be smart, to be clean, when he heard the news. Almost as if he was expecting his father to be here today. He would want Yossi to be smart and clean.

Of course, Yossi knew that his father would not

arrive today. Nobody would be reunited today. But they might have news. Maybe even letters. Some sort of communication.

Leo, Mordecai and Yossi strode across the sports field believing that today was the day that some of them would find out great news.

There was hope. There was excitement. That is what Yossi felt. That today he could have news of his father and the future could begin.

The same woman from the Red Cross was waiting to speak to them. She was wearing the same navy blue dress and the same kind expression on her face.

As the last children came into the hall, a silence fell as all three hundred waited to hear news of their families.

"Good morning, children," the Red Cross lady began. "After intense searching and checking and

cross-referencing, using your lists of names, it is with immense regret that I have to tell you the results of the meticulous research the Red Cross has been doing on your behalf ..."

Yossi stared at the woman as she went on talking. But he could not hear much of what she said. He needed to tell her that there had been a mistake. When she suggested that they prepare themselves for the strong possibility that nobody from their families had survived, Yossi shook his head. He wasn't going to prepare himself for that. His father was alive. He had to be.

The boys filed out of the hall in silence and walked off, each of them alone.

Was that it?

Yossi went to the lake. He needed to look across the water at the woodlands on the far shore, skeletal now with most of the leaves having blown away.

But his eyes were drawn higher, to the tops of the mountains, covered in their first dusting of winter snow. A stiff wind was coming from the north, up and over the mountains, bringing the cold with it. The same wind he had felt less than half an hour ago as he went excitedly to hear news about his father.

The lake looked huge and dull. No colour. It looked dead.

Yossi sat on a rock and glared out at the far shore. There was no news of his father. No record of his father trying to trace him. It didn't mean his father was dead, but it was a blow. A huge blow.

He stared hard into the small waves lapping up the beach. Traces of frost from the morning still clung to the rocks around the shore. He heard something above him and gazed into the huge sky. High, high above them a skein of geese was heading south-east.

Yossi followed the geese as they moved over the

estate until his eyes were drawn to a figure walking up the shore from the south.

A man. Carrying a large bulky bag.

It was hard to make out much more because his figure was so dark against the bright water, but he looked, with the large bag, to be a soldier. Yossi knew this was no soldier to fear. He felt safe in England now.

What kept Yossi's attention was the way the man was looking around himself, wild-eyed, across the lake, then into the trees, as if he was searching for something.

He came closer and closer, reminding Yossi of Joyce's dad, who still worked at the flying boat factory. But too young to be him.

Yossi stood up.

He gasped in a great gulp of air.

"Peter?" he called.

The man stopped and stared at Yossi, his long rough brown kitbag dropping to his side.

"Yes," the young man said, guarded.

Yossi thought hard about what he should say now. Here was Dorothy's son, Peter, back from the war, looking for his family.

"I know you," Yossi said.

"Me? You know me?"

"I mean ..." Yossi was doing his best to speak clear English. "I know your family. I know where they live. Your mother."

"Yes," Peter nodded, now talking fast and urgent. "Are they all well? My mother? My father? Little Joyce? I haven't seen them since I left Liverpool."

"They are all well," Yossi said gently, understanding that Peter had never been here before. His family had moved from Liverpool while he

was fighting in the Far East. That was why he looked so lost.

"Let me show you," Yossi offered.

"Please." Peter half-smiled.

"This way," Yossi said. Then they walked up from the shore along the line of the beck. Peter didn't say a word, so Yossi decided not to ask any questions.

"It's just this way," Yossi coaxed.

Peter followed, still silent.

The closer he came to Joyce's house, the more Yossi could feel himself trembling with emotion. He wasn't sure what he was about to face.

To reunite a mother, a father and a sister with the son and brother they feared was dead. That would be hard.

The emotions would be overpowering.

This is what he had wanted so badly for himself.

How would he cope seeing a father and son reunited? Part of him felt like running away. He wasn't sure he could handle it, wasn't sure how it would play out. But he stiffened himself against his fears. He would do this. It was a good thing to do. He owed Dorothy and her family so much for their hospitality and kindness. He could do this one thing, then slip away, couldn't he?

They walked on, within sight of the house now.

"That's your mother's house," Yossi told Peter, pointing. "The one with the trellis around the door where the roses grow in the summer."

Yossi stared hard at the window where he knew Dorothy would be standing, keeping an eye out along the main road as always.

He saw movement.

And then she was there, standing with her cloth in one hand, her other hand on the door frame. She

looked to Yossi as if she might fall. Until she dropped
her cloth on the floor and began to rush down
the street towards them, the figure of a small girl
running behind her.

NINETEEN

Yossi left Joyce's household to their family reunion.
It was personal. Better to leave them to their joy
without having to worry about guests.

Word had got round. Leo and Mordecai soon
heard about the arrival of the young man. They
found Yossi near the lake, where he told them what
had happened and how he had led Peter to his
mother.

In witnessing the reunion of Joyce's family,
Yossi had decided the future.

His future.

Maybe their future, he hoped.

Seeing that family who loved each other so much had settled Yossi's mind.

At first the three boys walked in silence. With the frosts and wind over the last few days, there had been a huge leaf fall, as if all the leaves in the woods had come down at once to carpet the twisted roots and wet soil below. It was heavy going. But still none of them spoke.

Yossi knew they could tell he had something to say. He knew they would wait until he spoke. They were close. They could read each other. That was part of the reason behind what he wanted to say to them.

After walking as far as the flying-boat factory, they sat on the rocks each of them always sat on. Yossi stared out and took a deep breath. Then he began.

"What do you want to do when we leave, Mordi?" he asked.

"So this is the conversation?" Leo interrupted.

"Yes," Yossi said.

Mordecai pressed his lips together so that they turned white.

"If you two came with me," Mordecai said, looking at his hands, then up to the faces of Leo and Yossi, "then we would go to Leeds and I would study and you two would do something you want to do. But that is only if you two come with me. If not, I don't know."

Yossi nodded.

He saw Leo leaning forwards, ready to say his piece.

"Me next, Leo," Yossi said.

"Who made you boss?" Leo asked.

"I did," Yossi replied, staring his friend out.

Leo shrugged, then smirked.

"I ..." Yossi began, "I know there is a chance

that I am not going to find my father. Not for a while. We have to leave Calgarth soon. Look, it's winter."

Yossi's two friends stared at him, speechless. This was a big change for him. His story had always been to find his father. That is all they had ever expected from him.

"I looked at Joyce's family back then," Yossi went on. "They have each other. We have no families. But ..."

"... we have each other now," Mordecai said.

"So you'd go to Leeds with Mordi?" Leo asked Yossi.

Yossi nodded, looking hard into Leo's eyes, hoping that he would not be upset that he did not share the dream of going to Palestine. He saw Leo chewing the insides of his cheek, thinking.

"Fine," Leo said at last.

Mordecai jumped up off his stone, his voice breaking. "You mean you would? You will?"

Leo nodded.

Now their eyes were on Yossi, who hesitated, momentarily distracted by a droning noise.

"We're agreed then," Yossi said. "Leeds. Together."

The three boys sat in silence and shared tight smiles as the background noise became louder. Yossi, his body angled away from the lake, was the last to see it. But he knew what it was from the look of wonder on his friends' faces.

He turned to see that he was right, as a Short Sunderland seaplane began to move slowly up the lake towards the Calgarth Estate.

At first it seemed like a large boat with wings, the wake behind it a white line scored up Windermere. But then, Yossi noticed, its nose seemed

to push downwards as if it was going to go under the water, not above it.

The wings wobbled to one side, then the other.

Would it get off the water? Could it take off, really?

But then Yossi took in a huge breath as the enormous plane somehow began to lift into the air.

For a few seconds there was a tiny gap – maybe a metre – between the flying boat and the surface of the lake, a storm of waves and water filling it. Yossi wondered if it really would take off. It was almost as if the water of the lake wanted to drag it back down.

Then he remembered what Jock Lawrence's brother had said: the aeroplane keeps going, building up more and more power before it can lift off. It takes time, but once it has enough power, it leaves the ground.

And then the seaplane was airborne – clearly

airborne. Yossi joined his friends, grinning and breaking into spontaneous wild applause as the aeroplane moved upwards, then turned to fly low over the trees and the cluster of houses and hostels of the Calgarth Estate.

Now Yossi knew that aeroplanes *could* take off. However heavy they were and whatever there was trying to drag them down, they could leave the surface of the water or the ground and fly anywhere they wanted to.

Yossi glanced at his two friends – Leo and Mordecai – and he knew that, if they stuck together, perhaps they too could find the power to prevent those invisible forces from dragging them down.

Some of the 300 children in Prague before their flight to the UK.

Settling in to life on the Calgarth Estate.

A MESSAGE FROM TOM PALMER

As you can imagine, this was a difficult book to write. The Holocaust was a horrific event, but it is something we must continue to think about and talk about even now, seventy-five years after the end of the Second World War.

It is very important to me, when I am writing about history, that I represent what really happened as accurately as possible – especially out of respect for the people who suffered the events that I am describing. The only way I felt that I could write *After the War* honestly was to base every scene on real events and the memories of the Windermere Boys.

But, saying that, Yossi, Leo and Mordecai are not real people. They are *composite characters*, meaning their stories of the Holocaust were drawn from the experiences of several of the Windermere Boys.

During my research I spent hours talking to historians who have been working with Holocaust survivors, including the Windermere Boys. The book has

been checked by those historians to make sure I have got my facts right. But any errors that remain are mine.

When I listen to Holocaust survivors, they often say that they are speaking publicly in order to ensure that their story will not be forgotten and in the hope that such terrible events can never happen again. Once I became aware of the Windermere Boys, that is what motivated me: to carry on telling their story and ensure that it is not forgotten.

The Calgarth Estate in the 1940s.

At the cinema.

At school on the Calgarth Estate.

THE HOLOCAUST

In *After the War*, we see some of the children burn an effigy of a man called Adolf Hitler. Adolf Hitler was the leader of Germany and of the Nazi Party.

Hitler and the Nazis were racist and antisemitic. They wrongly believed that Jewish people were a race that was both dangerous and sub-human. The Nazis incorrectly blamed Jews for Germany losing the First World War and believed that the country would be a better, stronger place if they could get rid of them.

During the Second World War, when Nazi Germany invaded and took over other countries, like Poland, they wanted to get rid of the Jews living there too. By the end of 1941, the Nazis, helped by many thousands of other people from across Europe, had begun to murder Jewish men, women and children. This mass murder of the Jews of Europe would continue until the defeat of the Nazis at the end of the war and it has become known as the Holocaust.

During the Holocaust, the Nazis and their collaborators were responsible for the murder of around 6 million Jewish people in Europe. Nearly seven out of every ten Jews in Europe were killed just because of who they were.

The Nazis also targeted other groups, including gay people, Roma ("gypsies"), disabled people and those who disagreed with their political views. Many millions of people from these other groups were also murdered.

The Holocaust became known as a genocide – the deliberate killing of a group of people because of their nationality, race or religion. On 27 January every year, people mark Holocaust Memorial Day and believe that it is important never to forget this terrible crime against humanity.

VISIT *AFTER THE WAR* ON WWW.TOMPALMER.CO.UK

The *After the War* page on Tom's website features a wealth of resources for teachers, librarians and parents to use to help children engage with this book and the broader subject of the Holocaust and the Second World War.

It includes:

- short films made by the author explaining the book and his writing process, made in Poland and the English Lake District;

- articles and blogs about how to write a story set in a historical period and how to research history;

- free posters for your classroom or library;

- a range of printable classroom resources, including a cover prediction exercise and others;

- information about Tom Palmer's school and library visits, where he can talk about *After the War* – around Holocaust Memorial Day and throughout the year.

Tom has written many historical novels, including *Armistice Runner*, *Over the Line* and *FlyBoy*, set in the First World War, and *D-Day Dog* and *Spitfire*, set in the Second World War. Each of those books has its own webpage on **tompalmer.co.uk**.

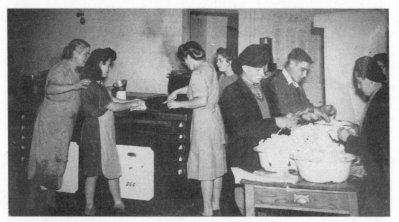

Children and staff in the kitchen at Calgarth.

One of the football teams at Calgarth.

ACKNOWLEDGEMENTS

Every scene in this book is based on the recollection of real events that I have listened to, read about or spoken to Holocaust experts about. In some cases I have heard accounts from the survivors themselves.

I have researched the stories meticulously for months, visiting Windermere, Auschwitz and Theresienstadt amongst other places. I have had the expert guidance of several people and organisations along the way, and the book has been checked by many, including historians and the families of some of the children who were there when these events happened.

Trevor Avery and Rosemary Smith from the Lake District Holocaust Project gave me hours of their time and the opportunity to meet some of the survivors and hear their stories first hand. I even joined them in an archaeological dig on the former site of the Calgarth Estate. They introduced me to some of the Windermere children, whom I was lucky to speak with: Arek Hersh, Mala Tribich and Ike Alterman. Thank you also to Kim and Judy from the '45 Aid Society for their excellent input. The '45 Aid Society is the charity established by all 732 survivors who came to the UK as part of the same scheme that brought the Windermere Boys; it is now run by their families.

You can visit the Lake District Holocaust Project exhibition at Windermere Library in Cumbria, and visit their website at **www.ldhp.org.uk**.

I spent a lot of time talking with Joyce and Marion, both of whom lived on the Calgarth Estate as children, Joyce during the events described in the book. I am hugely grateful to both. Joyce appears in the story along with her dog, Spot.

Thanks too to Ailsa Bathgate, my editor at Barrington Stoke, for her guidance and sensitivity. David Luxton, my agent, for looking after me on and off the page. Simon Robinson, my friend, who read the book at least three times and gave me candid feedback. Clare Zinkin, Valda Varadinek and Sarah Middleton for reading the book and making invaluable contributions. And to the teachers and children at Menston Primary School.

I owe a lot to my wife for reading the book through in its various stages and putting up with my obsession with the topic and the mood swings I went through while writing it. It was my wife's idea that I should write about the Windermere Boys, after hearing a BBC Radio programme about them.

My final thank you is to the children of Grasmere School who read a late version of the book and gave me some great feedback. They wanted to know more about what happened to the Jewish children during the Holocaust. They said they wanted to know the clear facts, so that they could understand what had happened.

I hope I have done that for them, because that has to be the main reason for writing about events like these.